His grip began to struggle...

"What a little coward you are," he said harshly. "You can't act the hysterical little virgin forever. Get to know about life instead of running away from it."

"That's what all seducers say," she hurled at him. "I'm telling you, Nick Langford, touch me and I'll scream!"

"Of course, you could, but you won't." He pinned her glistening head with his hand. "The truth is, you little witch, you've been trying to bring me around to kissing you for some time."

"You crazy man!" Sheer rage overcame Kendall's fear and she threw back her head. "Oh, you—damned men! Listen here, you conceited oaf...."

His mouth covered hers completely, stilling her protest and stealing away her quaking breath.

MARGARET WAY
is also the author of these
Harlequin Romances

and these
Harlequin Presents

Many of these titles are available at your local bookseller.

For a free catalogue listing all available Harlequin Romances and Harlequin Presents, send your name and address to:

HARLEQUIN READER SERVICE
M.P.O. Box 707, Niagara Falls, NY 14302
Canadian address: Stratford, Ontario N5A 6W2

Flamingo Park

by

MARGARET WAY

Harlequin Books

TORONTO • LONDON • LOS ANGELES • AMSTERDAM
SYDNEY • HAMBURG • PARIS • STOCKHOLM • ATHENS • TOKYO

Original hardcover edition published in 1980
by Mills & Boon Limited

ISBN 0-373-02400-2

Harlequin edition published April 1981

Printed in U.S.A.

CHAPTER ONE

Oh, it was hot! A scorcher. She would wait another ten minutes, then take the beetle down to the beach. The afternoon had been a spectacular success. She had sold every last hand of lady finger bananas, most of the pineapples, pawpaws and watermelons, all of the avocados and a wide selection of her little potted plants. It was amazing, her green finger, and in her family, rare.

Many times her father said to her, "You amaze me, darling, the way you understand plants. What is it you do, speak to them?"

She did. Sometimes she whistled or sang. The plants seemed to like it. Her father didn't understand plants. He was a painter, a good one, who had bought the farm with the quaint notion that he only had to sit there for everything to grow.

Poor Harry! This week he was in Sydney trying to drum up another agent. Pamela had thoroughly antagonised the last one, to the extent that he had finally blazed out of the house in a rage. Kendall could remember the evening vividly; the way the dinner had stuck in her throat. Pamela had many unfortunate talents and an abiding aspiration to be the wife of a famous artist. It was pathetic really, Pamela's ambitions and cold reality.

Kendall sighed and leaned back precariously in her chair. Through the great crimson tresses of the poinciana above her she could see burning blue chunks of the sky. It reminded her of the sea, that heavenly dense blue. The surf would be flat. There wasn't even a

breeze to stir the air and long tendrils of her hair had
escaped its fat topknot to curl damply on her bare
shoulders.

There just had to be a storm; they invariably sprang
up late afternoon. Not that she cared. On the whole,
she enjoyed storms—spectacular storms that lived on
in the memory. Tropical Queensland was her home, and
she never wanted to live anywhere else. Since she had
made that choice, it all seemed easier.

Despite the languorous heat, she felt as strong and
thriving as all her little plants. People who loved nature
had only to use their eyes to find a whole world of peace
and comfort and strength. Here, everything flowered so
brilliantly—the jacarandas, the tulip trees, the towering
poincianas that made the crater road such a glorious
place for an afternoon's drive. There were cassias too,
spilling gold everywhere, the varying pinks of the crêpe
myrtles and oleanders and all the hundred and one
smaller trees like the fragrant frangipani and the creamy
mock orange. Kendall adored beauty, exotica, the
drowsy contentment of the molten golden heat. It suited
her just like it suited Harry. He had always hungered
after beauty.

Poor Harry! Pamela had filled his eyes and clouded
his wisdom.

A huge black monster of a mosquito was feeding on
the smooth skin of her leg and she leaned down non-
chalantly and swiped it flat. The hazards didn't bother
her; the cyclones, the snakes, the myriad biting insects.
Of course she had plenty of skin showing, dressed for
the heat, in brief shorts and an even briefer bra top, but
at eighteen, with a flawless young figure, such manner
of dress looked extraordinarily attractive.

In another five minutes, if the Flanagan kids didn't
pass by, she would pack up what was left and take it
back to the house. At least she wouldn't have the awful
job of lifting the whole lot back into the trunk again.

The watermelons had almost defeated her. Still, there was satisfaction in knowing Pamela wouldn't be too proud to pocket the proceeds. No matter how often and loudly she deplored Kendall's "disgusting little hawker act," every little bit helped. It wasn't for Pamela to lower herself by sitting at the front gate selling fruit and plants. Such vulgarities were only for Kendall, or Harry when he felt like it.

The truth was, they were rather short on money until Harry found himself a good agent, one who had the sense not to come to dinner. In the days of Benjii, the farm had flourished. Then Pamela had taken it into her shining head to call him a "dirty little kanaka" and Benjii had come no more. Benjii was a descendant of a Gilbert Islander who had been blackbirded to work in the canefields, but Benjii was a gentleman, kind and hard-working. Kendall had begged him, Harry had begged him to stay, but Benjii had a high sense of dignity. Mrs. Reardon was as beautiful as a goddess, but he had no wish to ever again hear the sound of her voice.

After Benjii the farm just seemed to slide into a wilderness. The earth still bore prolifically and Harry found the wild jungle tangle exciting until snakes started to get into the house. Benjii had warned her about that. She often saw him in town and they talked about everything except Pamela. Benjii's son Ellis had been in High School with Kendall, a straight A student now in his second year of engineering at the Queensland University. Benjii had slaved like his great-grandfather to give his son a chance. Kendall had been a straight A student too, but Harry hadn't been able to help her with fees and all the extra expense of dressing and boarding away from home. It had been quite impossible for her to go to university like Ellis.

She closed her eyes and felt the hot sting of tears. So what? Another hope blasted. Harry was luckier than he deserved, but she loved him. Besides, he needed her. She

knew and he knew. Even Pamela needed her as a house-
maid. To put a stop to her thoughts, she jumped up
and folded her chair into the trunk. She didn't fancy
going back to the house. Pamela had been decidedly irritable with Harry gone, but there was nothing
else for it. Anyway, a swim would make up for sacri-
ficing the whole afternoon. Tomorrow would be
Monday and work again as usual. It wasn't a disaster being assistant to the secretary of the Mill
Manager. All she had to do was hold back her own feelings.

She didn't see the panel van flash by, but she heard
the squeal of brakes as it went into a U-turn and roared
back.

"Anything for me, love? I'm hungry."

His two hands were resting on the steering wheel and
he was leaning sideways looking out the window. He
was about her age, with long blond hair hanging down
either side of a sharp-featured, rather good-looking
face. His eyes were a pale blue and unreached by his
smile.

"What can you afford to buy?" Despite her cool,
businesslike tone, she felt her heart begin to race.

"Let's see what you've got?" Already he was out of
the van and to her surprise, because she hadn't seen him
at all, he was joined by another youth in tattered jeans
hacked off below the knee.

"It's incredible, really," Fair Hair was saying slowly,
"to find you on a back road."

The way he was staring at her was rattling her composure, but she wasn't going to let him see it. "It's busy,
though," she said briskly. "Lots of people visit the
lake."

"You're too pretty to be safe." He picked up a pawpaw and put it down again.

"You're joking," she said dryly. "You haven't seen
Sebastian yet."

Both of them thought about that and Fair Hair frowned and looked around. "Sebastian?"

"My dog," Kendall retorted. "A German shepherd."

"Where is he, then?"

"He comes if I whistle. Don't make me feel like it."

"Keep your cool." There was mockery in the thin, tanned face. "We're not doing anything, are we?"

"The watermelons are good," Kendall said matter-of-factly, trying to dispel the tension.

"Are they? That's better."

"You grow 'em?" Tattered Jeans spoke—rather shrilly, Kendall thought.

"My father does." The way Kendall said it, it sounded as if Harry was a gigantic farmhand.

"And how is he spending his holiday?" Fair Hair picked up a watermelon, rattled it, then handed it to his companion, who staggered a little under the weight, then walked away to put it in the van.

"Well?" The pale blue eyes slid over her and their expression made her skin crawl.

"Might as well ask him. He'll be here in a minute."

"The classic bit of jazz for little girls on their own." He smiled at her as if to show he liked her little show of bravado. "My name's Bones. That's Foxy." He pointed to his friend.

"He's charming," Kendall returned offensively, but she was losing her temper. These two delightful louts were out for some innocent little pleasure. Like pushing her into their van. If she let them. If she could just get her hands on a watermelon she would smash it over their heads. A pot plant would do. It had been a mistake letting Colin take Sebastian off to the beach. Usually he sat watch beside her, half asleep, half alert, but always formidable.

Fair Hair suddenly leaned forward and pulled a long strand of her hair, his eyes flickering as it ran like silk through his calloused fingers. "You're beautiful, do you know that? In the best way of all—young and wild."

Instinctively she had jerked her head back and her
scalp tingled with the pain. "If you've got some kind of
plan," she said sharply, "forget it. I'm absolutely not
interested."

"Are you sure about that?" His hand fell to the curve
of her shoulder, exploring the bone.

"Hey, Bones!" Tattered Jeans called to him urgently.
"There's a car comin' up. Fancy—a big Jag."

"That's my friend." Relief made Kendall's voice
high. "He's a cop."

"Cops don't ride in Jags, girlie."

"It's his day off." She felt almost lightheaded. Far
better a lecture from Nick than an unwelcome ride. Fair
Hair had released her and stepped back a few paces, his
expression wary.

The dark green Jaguar swept on ahead, then executed
a smooth silent turn and purred back.

"See, you two, you should really listen." Kendall had
never been so pleased to see Nick in her life.

He got out of his car and came towards them, the
man of action, big and tough with an all-engulfing aura
of money and power.

"What goes on?" he asked grimly.

"Nothing, Nick." Kendall gave a cheeky smile. She
could afford to, now.

"So you know these two?" His brilliant black eyes
flashed contempt.

"We just stopped to buy a watermelon." Fair Hair
spoke carefully, with just a trace of petulance.

"Have you got it?" There was a crackle in Nick's
clipped voice.

"Just put it on the front seat." Fair Hair looked to
Foxy for confirmation and the other nodded.

"Pay for it?"

"Not yet." Fair Hair shook his head and fumbled in
his pocket. "How much?"

"Only as much as everyone else," said Kendall. "A dollar."

"Pass it over and go." Nick held out his hand. "If you step on it you'll make Stony Creek before dark. That's where you're going, isn't it?"

"I told you, you shouldn't have stopped!" Tattered Jeans, who had stood silently, suddenly erupted wrathfully.

"I can't imagine why you didn't listen." Nick handed the crumpled note to Kendall. "What all three of us aren't admitting, I'm good at guessing."

"So all right, we're going." Pale blue eyes glistened with futile rage.

"Do that." Nick brought his hand down hard on the young man's shoulder and turned him towards the van.

"Oh, gosh!" Kendall was left to moan to herself. As if Nick needed another reason to lecture her! She looked back and saw both young men were now in the van. Nick was leaning his two hands against the door of the driver's seat, his black head bent as he told them to haul off. He might just as well have been a policeman for the way they obeyed.

When they were safely away, Fair Hair put his head out the window and called a few words that made Kendall gasp.

"Terrific!" she said wryly.

"Well, what did you expect from a couple of louts?" Nick had come back to her looking down at her angrily. "Didn't I warn you about something like this?"

"You did." She tilted her chin.

"So the sooner you ditch the idea of sitting out here every weekend, the better."

"Not when I've got more than a hundred dollars to show for it."

"They could have taken that away from you as well," he pointed out, his tone oddly harsh.

"No, really, Nick—" she tried to placate him.

"Hell, you don't have to lie about it!" His handsome mouth thinned. "I don't like to think about what might have happened if I hadn't come along. Where's Sebastian, anyway? I thought I told you to keep him close at hand?"

"Colin took him to the beach," she explained offhandedly. "So what do you want me to do, buy a gun?"

"I think you can let Harry do this kind of thing in future," he returned curtly. "Or your boy-friend when he can get away from Mother. You're no ugly duckling. A man would have to be feeble and blind not to notice you in that get-up."

"It wasn't intentional." She flushed under his sweeping gaze.

"I know that. I don't think you notice anything you put on."

"So what?" For some reason she was absurdly hurt. "It takes money to keep up with the fashions."

"Pamela seems to manage," he pointed out.

"She's the beauty in the family."

He narrowed his eyes briefly, and looked straight down at her. "Not my opinion exactly."

"Who, then—Sebastian?" She held herself defiantly straight, he was so darn tall.

"That's right."

He was the same as usual; mocking, aggressive, Big Brother, yet different. Whatever it was, Kendall wasn't ready for it. Nick Langford and his all-knowing, all-seeing eyes.

"And when's Harry coming back?" He seemed to sense her discomfort.

"As soon as he finds another agent." She gave a little grimace, still unable to put Rudy Mayer out of her mind.

"In the meantime he lets his pint-sized little daughter put herself in danger."

"You *like* Harry. Admit it," she said passionately.

"Sure I do." He sounded cool. "I just don't like what's happening to you."

"Well, thanks for the kind thoughts!" Her clear young voice was tinged with sarcasm. "What brings you here anyway?"

"Is it essential for you to know?"

"Just conversation." She moved to pick up some pot plants and he put her firmly out of the way.

"You're a challenging little thing, aren't you?" he asked a bit tightly. "Where do you want these, in the trunk?"

"Thank you."

"It *is* something you can say it. Why is it young Hogan isn't here helping you? I thought you two were inseparable."

"He must have some relaxation," she retorted belligerently. "I told him to go." And she had.

"Not you?" Nick glanced back at her, small and slender, her golden-skinned face flushed apricot over the cheekbones.

"I manage."

"You can't go on managing," he said brutally.

"So what am I supposed to do?" she stamped the ground with her sandalled foot, "let everything rot to the ground?" In a small frenzy she bent down and picked up a huge watermelon.

"Give that to me!" he hissed through his teeth.

Still she resisted until he slapped her hand away. "If you must know, Nick Langford, I'm a lot stronger than I look."

"So why are you trembling?"

"That's *you*!" she burst out wrathfully. "You'd have made Boadicea tremble in her boots."

"She couldn't have had as many prickles as you." He turned his broad back on her and began to stow the rest of the produce away in the trunk. "If you let me, I can help you a lot."

"I can't do that, Nick." It came out as little more than a whisper . "The farm belongs to Harry."

"Harry won't mind. It's you who's always been the rebel." He looked at her levelly, but she wouldn't return his gaze.

"Things will be better if Harry sells a few paintings."

"He's not turning out enough," he pointed out deliberately. "Harry's the kind of man who needs driving along."

"For heaven's sake, Pamela does that."

"I feel sure she tries, but she's not having much success. It seems to me Harry has lost motivation. When you first came here his work was important to him, he had a young daughter to rear. Nowadays he's become surprisingly indolent."

"It's the climate," she said, and looked away.

"What's really wrong with Harry?" Unexpectedly he grasped her shoulders and held her to face him.

"I don't know." It was strange to have his hands on her bare skin. "I don't think he's really well."

"He drinks too much," Nick said bluntly.

"I suppose he does. I didn't expect you to notice."

"I've got eyes."

"So you have. Black as night!" She was surprised to see herself reflected in their brilliant depth. "You despise us, don't you, Nick?"

"Little fool!" He released her abruptly. "If you're really worried about Harry, you'll have to get him to see a doctor."

"Harry—*doctors*?" Despite herself her voice rose. "He won't see a doctor. He hasn't been near one in years, not since my mother died. She needn't have died, you know. A doctor failed to diagnose her condition and by the time another one did it was too late. Harry has never forgotten."

"Yet neither of you speak about her."

"What is there to say?" She was standing in a spear

of sunlight and it slanted across her suddenly vulnerable young face. "That we loved her and miss her dreadfully every day?"

"Poor baby!" There was a fascinating tenderness in his deep voice.

"I'm not a baby, Nick." She *had* to move away from him. "I'm eighteen years old."

"God, don't I know it!" he spoke crisply. "The problem is, how to protect you."

"With you, it seems to amount to a complex," she retorted.

"There are periods when I think so myself," he returned acidly. "What I really came this way for was to ask you all over to a party next Saturday night. I'll have some guests I have to entertain. Think Harry will be back?"

Kendall couldn't help smiling. "He'll come back especially just to please you."

"Harry's good company."

"He says the same of you. Good old Nick, witty, ironic, sharp and polished."

"You wouldn't put it like that?" His black eyes tried to take her apart.

"I don't understand you, like Harry."

"How in the world could you. A *baby*. Anyway, are you coming?"

"Oh yes, if you really want me." Her delicate dark brows drew together. "You don't have to ask me just because you ask Harry and Pamela."

"Beautifully put!" he said jeeringly. "When are you going to grow up?"

"I suppose I ought to," she sighed with sudden contrition.

"*I* think so." Nick tilted her chin with hard, hurting fingers. "Sometimes you sound like a very stupid little girl."

"Maybe you expect too much of me," she reproached

him. "Very well, Nick, I'd be delighted to come. I wish there were a few about my age."

"My God! " he was moved to exclaim. "You're the only female I know who makes me feel a good eighty years old. Shall I ask Colin for you? Your great pal?"

"Why are you so critical of Colin?" she demanded.

"It's born in me. I'm a very critical person."

"I assure you you are."

"Thanks again." He bowed suavely.

"Just because Colin—" she broke off abruptly, seeing his face tighten into boredom. "Oh what's the use? Colin's not quite the ninny you think. You simply don't understand his kind of person."

"I don't think I want to," he drawled with frightful contempt. "I'd admire him a whole lot more if he'd been here with you this afternoon. Incidentally, I'll have to mention the incident to Harry. You're taking too much of a risk doing what you're doing. These days there are too many drifters on the road, young men out of work who won't stop at anything."

"So you're a millionaire!" She stood squarely in front of him, feeling oddly lightheaded.

"I ought to smack you for that," he returned rather curtly.

"All right, I'm sorry." She reached out and laid a pleading hand on his arm. "Please, Nick, don't say anything to Harry. I promise I'll have Sebastian with me in future."

"Fine words, no parsnips buttered. That's what you told me the last time. Besides, even Sebastian isn't positive protection. Why can't you see yourself as others see you?"

"Oh, my goodness, as bad as that?" She tried to speak flippantly, knowing she was annoying him.

"If you kept at it, there'd be other incidents, believe me. It's a wonder you've been able to pull it off as long as you have. If you need the extra money,

Harry will have to do it himself or pay somebody else."

She looked no higher than his uncompromising cleft chin. "God, you're a bully!" she snapped.

"I am indeed."

"I swear I'll be careful, Nick."

"*No.*" He spoke with finality.

"All right, then," she looked instinctively back towards the house. "Are you coming up to the house?"

"Can I give you a lift?" he asked dryly.

"You know I want you to come."

Nick smiled briefly, without humour. "That's right, remember your manners."

"I tend to forget them when you're around," she swung around, half subdued.

"In any case, I have some cassettes for Pamela."

"Oh...she wanted some?"

He was moving back to his car, lithe and powerful. "She rang me when she knew I was going South."

"Nothing too much trouble for Nick Langford."

"Jealous?" He gave her a smile of great calculation and charm.

"How comical!" she drawled.

"Sarcastic little brat!"

"I had a good teacher."

He didn't answer but put a hard hand to her elbow. "Come along."

"Don't tell me you're going to try and drive my little bomb?" She looked up at him in amazement.

"Thank you, I'd like to." He whistled beneath his breath. "I bet it handles superbly."

"You'll get the hang of it...eventually."

He opened the door and Kendall slid in the passenger seat, watching while he crossed around the front of the little car and got in beside her. "Good God!" he said succinctly, "what do you do for head and leg room?"

"It must be a great problem being over six feet."

He pushed the seat back as far as it would go and looked at her. "Damn you, you little witch!"

"You can't be very bright." There was something very male and hostile in his expression.

"Don't witches have black hair and green eyes?" he challenged her.

"You sound as if you'd like to burn every last one."

He looked away from her and switched on the ignition. "Witches are bound to get a man in trouble."

"I must remember that." Her hair was tumbling all over the place so she pulled the few remaining pins out and let it cascade around her face in deep waves. There was no doubt about it, something about her got under Nick's skin. And if it did, she was the same about him. Nick had always made her feel bristly.

She didn't speak as they drove up to the house, but sat looking out at the wilderness of the garden and beyond. She knew exactly what Nick was thinking as he too looked about him, but mercifully he didn't say anything.

When he stopped the car she dashed out, slapping the mosquitoes from her beautiful, slender legs. "I'll just tell Pamela."

"All right," he nodded agreeably. "Where do you want me to put everything?"

"Oh, just under the house will do." She waved a vague hand and began to run up the front stairs. One simply couldn't walk in on Pamela without being announced.

She found her stepmother on the back patio, relaxing in Harry's planter chair. "So you're back?" Pamela asked without interest.

"Nick's here!" Kendall announced breathlessly.

"*What?*" Pamela literally leapt from the chair. "And I would look so goddam untidy!"

"You look perfect," Kendall assured her.

"Try and stall him for a few minutes," Pamela put a

fretful hand to her ash-blonde hair. "I'll have to change my dress."

"Don't be mad. Just come as you are."

"Nothing doing!" Pamela's blue eyes flashed their scorn. "Maybe you like going around like a gypsy, but I don't."

"Please yourself," Kendall turned away quickly. "Do you think he'll stay to tea?"

"I'm certainly going to ask him." Pamela looked disgusted with the question.

"Oh well, there's food." Not enough.

Kendall found Nick in the bush house staring at all her hanging baskets.

"Hi!" His easy smile caught her off balance, it was so attractive and friendly. "What's this one called?" He fingered some superbly scented pink flower clusters.

"South China Spring." She went to stand at his shoulder. "It's one of the Hoyas. If you like it, you can have it."

"Sure?" He considered her uplifted face.

"Yes."

"Frankly I'm overwhelmed," he told her.

"Do you want it or not?" She tore her eyes away from him with an effort, exasperated and she didn't know why. "It's nice to think I can give Nick Langford something he likes."

"As a matter of fact you can."

"Half a minute, we're still talking about the plant."

"What else?" He sounded surprised, though there was a sardonic twist to his mouth. "I have the very place for it."

"So now you're going to be kind?"

"Fancy!" He dropped a brotherly arm about her shoulders. "I guess now and again I regret the things I've said to you over the years."

Kendall looked up at him suspiciously, then smiled.

"Actually you were pretty nice to me when I was fourteen."

"Isn't it terrible to grow up!"

As they came up the stairs Pamela was standing on the landing, looking as though she was just about to be photographed for *Vogue*.

"Nick, how lovely to see you!" She put out her arms, rather effusively Kendall thought, but evidently Nick did not, for he took her two hands in his own and bent and kissed her cheek. "You look stunning, Pamela. As always."

"One tries." She was smiling brilliantly, feeding on a man's admiration. "Do come in and have a drink. I was just thinking of coming for Kendall when you arrived. If you only knew how I worry about that girl!"

Bunkum! Kendall thought to herself solemnly. Pamela had never worried about anyone but herself in her life.

"If you'll excuse me, I'll have a quick shower and change," she excused herself diplomatically. The sooner Pamela had Nick to herself the better.

"Take your time, I'm in no hurry." To prove it, Nick dropped into the armchair Kendall had recently covered.

"It seems such a *long* time since we saw you last," Pamela said smilingly. "Explain."

Pamela had always been avid for Nick's company. Even Harry had noticed that.

In the bathroom, Kendall stripped off her clothes, pulled the shower cap over her hair and stepped under the wonderfully cold jet of water. Colin was expecting her down at the beach, but after a while he would realise she wasn't coming. Colin had wanted to stay and help her, but she had talked him out of it. He needed a break, he worked hard enough during the week.

Later she towelled herself dry and lifting her head encountered her own reflection in the wall mirror. Why suddenly *see* herself at this precise minute? She dropped the pink towel and just stood there looking at herself warily.

Why don't you see yourself as others see you?

She found herself remembering Nick's words and the terse way he had put them, so she regarded herself sombrely, as though she were a piece of inanimate sculpture.

She wasn't flamboyantly beautiful like Pamela; tall, full-breasted, long-stemmed and voluptuous, but there was nothing wrong with her body either, even if it was slightly too small and slender. She reached for her robe and stared at her face. Harry always said she had a lot of character in her face. Did she? She was certainly not mousey. All her features were very clearly defined; large eyes, curvy mouth, good bones. Pamela was always telling her she should pluck her eyebrows, but Harry said that was crazy. Her brows and lashes gave great definition to her green eyes. Her mother's eyes and mouth and the texture of her olive skin. Even her black hair was thick and heavy with a good natural wave.

After a minute it seemed to her kinky to be staring at herself, so she turned away hurriedly and walked into her bedroom. Her hair was quite damp, and damp it was inclined to become unruly. It really needed cutting and shaping, but the best hairdresser in town charged too damned much. Only one of the Langford women could afford to go there.

When she looked at herself again, she was wearing a jade-coloured camisole top and her best skirt; multicoloured hibiscus on a black ground. Her skin needed no gilding, but she put a bit of lip gloss on her mouth. At least it made her look older and more interested in her appearance. Nick's remark still rankled.

When she rejoined the others, Pamela was already playing one of the new cassettes, turning it down low so it wrapped them in sweet sound.

"Oh, it is good to see you, Nick," Pamela was still enthusing, arranged gracefully on the settee facing their visitor. "I've been bored stiff!"

"Never mind, Harry should be back this week." Nick stood up and glanced at Kendall, his eyes taking in her appearance in an instant. "What are you having, little one?"

"Anything." She glanced back at the expensive bar Harry had had put in. "Soda water, squash, anything, just so long as it's cold."

He poured squash over some ice and put a tiny splash of gin in it. "Here, you deserve something after putting in such a hot afternoon."

"She *will* do it!" Pamela clicked her tongue and looked at her stepdaughter with wry affection. "Still, young girls need a little extra pocket money—but I have a suspicion she's buying things for her box."

"My *what*?" Kendall turned her head in astonishment.

"Don't worry, darling," Pamela gave her rich little chuckle, "I think Nick knows you and Colin are going steady."

"Then he knows more than I do," she said abruptly. "I have no intention of getting married for years yet. I'm not looking for trouble."

"Oh, come now, darling, no one could call Colin trouble," Pamela said archly, "but we don't intend to tease you. Sit down."

From then on Pamela took charge of the conversation, making frequent laughing allusions to how "tame" it was, two women alone at the farm.

"Then why don't you allow me to take you both out to dinner?" Nick asked, with seemingly unforced gallantry.

"Not for me, Nick, thank you all the same," Kendall said hurriedly, embarrassed at how thickly Pamela had been piling it on. "Colin's bringing Sebastian back."

"So does that kill the whole evening?"

Almost on cue, there was a commotion at the front door and a magnificent German shepherd, weighing a good eighty pounds, bounded into the room.

"Darling!" Kendall put out her hand not only to welcome her much loved and devoted companion but to curb the dog's exuberance.

"You don't call guard dogs *darling,*" Nick said, half chiding, half indulgent.

"*I* do." Sebastian was standing poised with his front legs on her chair and his tail wagging ecstatically while Kendall patted his handsome head and pulled his ears.

"You know I hate the dog in the house, Kendall," Pamela's affectionate stepmamma façade was crumbling."

"I'm sorry, I'll put him outside. Colin is probably here."

Colin was at the front door, almost timidly peering in. "Oh, there you are, Kendall!" His thin face lit up. "You had me worried when you didn't turn up at the beach."

"Nick came along," she explained hastily, and had to drag Sebastian to put him out the front door. "Come in and say hello."

"Oh—" Colin glanced down at his T-shirt and board shorts as though he wasn't ready for such a major social encounter, then shrugged philosophically and moved into the hallway. "You look nice," he told Kendall with a look of adoration she missed. "What's the occasion?"

"I just felt like changing my image a little." She walked ahead of him into the living room.

"Hi!" Nick stood up lazily and put out his hand.

"How are you, Mr. Langford?" Colin shook the proffered hand and glanced respectfully at Pamela, reclining like an odalisque. "Mrs. Reardon."

Pamela nodded graciously. "I suppose you missed Kendall down at the beach."

"I was worried." Pamela waved her hand and Colin sat down quietly as if he were a child instead of a young man of twenty-four who had inherited a small, thriving farm.

"That's because you're already in her clutches," Pamela teased.

"Which isn't at all bad," Nick commented laconically. "Aren't you going to offer Colin a drink, Kendall?"

"What's it to be?" Kendall glanced down at Colin's silky, light brown hair.

"Oh—anything." He glanced up at her with the rather bewildered air of a young man whose parents totally disapproved of alcoholic beverages.

Kendall helped him out. "Have a lemon squash with me."

"That would be perfect!" Colin's cautious expression smoothed out.

"How's your mother, Colin?" Nick asked kindly, seemingly catching the drift of Colin's thoughts.

"A tower of strength, as always." Colin flashed the older man a grateful glance. "But I know she's missing Dad."

"I'm sure. It isn't that long."

"No." Colin sighed and hung his head.

"Now, now, snap out of it," Pamela bade him with breezy callousness, "aren't you taking Kendall out tonight?"

"No. . ." for an instant Colin looked confused, "that is, we haven't made any plans." Kendall handed him his drink and he met her wry glance. "I thought you said you were having an early night?"

"So I did," she said evenly. "Pamela must have forgotten."

"Then it looks like you and me, Nick." Pamela threw him a gleaming, triumphant glance. "These are liberated times. A woman doesn't have to feel embarrassed seen out without her husband."

"It wouldn't be Mother's view," Colin exclaimed piously, then flushed at his tactlessness. "I don't mean anything, of course, Mrs. Reardon."

"Well, we all know your mamma," Pamela smiled at him tigerishly, "but I for one could do with a night out."

"Obviously Kendall thinks you could do with a chaperone too," Nick glanced up to catch Kendall's betraying expression. "I suggest we all go somewhere quiet and relaxed and for Kendall's sake come home reasonably early."

"Sounds great!" Colin's sherry-brown eyes lit up. "What about the Golf Club?"

"The Golf Club it is," Nick confirmed suavely, and looked at Kendall as though daring her to disappoint Colin. "I have a jacket in the car, so I won't have to go home."

"Well, I shall have to." Colin took another sip of his drink, then stood up. "Mother won't mind. She's having a few of her old cronies over to play cards."

"Marvellous, it's wonderful to be encircled by friends!" Pamela came to her feet, five feet nine before she even put on her shoes, built on classic, Junoesque lines and still, at a questionable thirty-eight, a very striking-looking woman. "Needless to say, I won't be wearing this."

"When I was just enjoying it too!" Nick slanted a glance over Pamela's jersey tunic, in riotous colours.

"But not quite the thing for dinner." She put one hand on her curvy hip and smiled down at him, incredibly lush and, to Kendall's disapproving eyes, outlandishly provocative.

"Shall I come back for you, Kendall?" Colin asked helpfully.

"Too far." Nick shook his head. "We'll meet you there in about an hour."

"Go on," Kendall urged Nick gently, "manage everyone!"

"I'm only thinking of all the quite unnecessary waste of gasoline."

"I suppose that's why you drive a Jag," she returned sweetly. "The twelve-cylinder, isn't it?"

"What would you suggest, scrap it?"

"Your beautiful car?" Pamela was watching them both with her pale blue eyes slitted like a wary cat's. "Kendall likes to plague you, doesn't she, Nick? I've told her before it's unbecoming, but she's got Harry's runaway tongue."

"Actually I'd be pretty happy to inherit it." Kendall went with Colin to the doorway. "Nick thinks Harry's jolly good company!"

Drat Pamela, she thought irritably. Now she would have to spend the whole evening watching Pamela trying to captivate Nick instead of acting like an old married lady.

"I suppose I shouldn't say this," Colin hissed confidentially, and went straight ahead, "but your stepmother always makes me feel a trifle uneasy."

"Then why accept the invitation?"

"You know the answer to that one," his brown eyes shone. "Any excuse to be with you. Besides, it was very good of Nick to ask me, an unimportant young farmer."

"Which doesn't mean either of us have to grovel," said Kendall with a great big grudge.

"I thought you liked him?" Colin struggled to understand.

"Oh, I do," she said oddly, "but he can be absolutely maddening at times." Sebastian bounded up to her and she stood there, stroking the dog's ears. "Give my regards to your mother."

Colin smiled uncertainly. "I will. We're hoping you'll be able to come over for tea one night next week."

Kendall didn't answer. Although Mrs. Hogan was never anything else but polite, she always felt a decided chill in her presence. Colin's mother had always been possessive of her only child, but never so much as now when she had been a widow for two years.

Colin drove away and she went back upstairs, feeling self-conscious and embarrassed. It was highly unlikely Nick wanted to take them anywhere at all.

Pamela waited until she rejoined them in the living room, then she excused herself smilingly, "Entertain Nick while I'm gone, dear. Give him another drink."

"Do you want one?" Kendall asked when Pamela had wafted out in a cloud of musky, womanly fragrance.

"No," he answered carelessly, intent on her face. "What's the matter?"

She couldn't sustain his brilliant glance. "Oh, nothing. I just feel a little depressed about something."

"Tell me."

"You'd only say something abrasive," she answered moodily.

"But you can take it," he jeered softly. "Much as I bother you, you've nearly always confided in me."

"Perhaps because you won't let me do anything else!" She sank down in Harry's big leather armchair for comfort, looking very young and fragile. "I don't think Colin's mother likes me, which really doesn't matter except Colin is such a good friend and it makes things a little awkward at times."

"Dear me!" Nick spoke disparagingly. "Is Colin's friendship so important to you?"

"Of course it is!" she said with more vehemence than she intended. "Colin is nice, kind and gentle, like poor Mr. Hogan. *He* liked me."

"Most men would," Nick remarked briefly. "The thing is, little one, Mrs. Hogan is frightened of losing

Colin to the kind of girl she couldn't manage. That way, she'd be losing Colin.''

"Losing Colin?" She jumped up in agitation, her skirt swirling. "Colin is just a friend!"

"But he wants to be so much more." Nick stood up purposefully and gave her a gentle push back into the chair. "Like a lover."

"No!"

"Have you honestly never noticed?"

"What's come over you, Nick?" She brushed her heavy hair aside. "Colin and I simply get on well together."

"It must be wonderful. How does he do it?" Nick straightened a crooked painting of Harry's and eyed it.

"Oh, shut up!" Kendall glanced up at his strong profile. "You always find a way to destroy my peace of mind."

"Really?" He rounded on her so swiftly he startled her into a strangled gasp. Then, before she was even aware of his intention, he had her around the waist lifting her bodily out of the chair.

"Nick?" She was one shivering mess of feverish pulsations.

"Don't lose your cool, baby." The handsome mouth was smiling, but there was a dangerous glint in his eyes.

"What are you doing?" she demanded.

"Shaking you up a little. I think it's about time."

"Well, it *isn't*!" She was wavering crazily between struggling and falling right into his arms. "Please let me go."

"Certainly." He set her steadily on her feet, his hands dropping away from her narrow waist. "I never realised such a little fire-eater could be so nervous. Do you always struggle when a man holds you?"

"A man *hasn't*!" She gave him a tortured, smouldering glance.

"Poor baby. I imagine I'll have to give you a few lessons in the gentle art of dalliance."

"Thank you, no!" For the life of her she couldn't make a joke of it, or pass the moment off. At eighteen she had been kissed quite a few times and nearly always enjoyed it, so it was incredible to think how she had panicked when Nick grasped her in a mock embrace. He was a devil and she felt like slapping his face, except—

He was watching her, rather sharply she thought, so she made a great effort to conceal her extraordinary tension. "Anyway, I've been kissed plenty of times, did you know that?"

"Then I must absolutely kiss you myself." The tone was lazy and mocking, yet she took a few steps in the opposite direction.

"Sometimes I hate you, Nick," she said crossly.

"I only said it to get a rise out of you. Frankly, I find it a dead bore kissing babies."

The phone rang out in the hallway and Kendall excused herself and fled.

It was Harry, and when she heard his dear, familiar voice, she nearly burst into overwrought tears.

"Daddy!" She hadn't called Harry Daddy in years—proof that she was shaken out of the norm.

"How's my girl?" Harry's bass-baritone boomed over the wires.

"Fine." When she had almost died of heart failure. "And you? We've been waiting anxiously for some news from you."

"And I've been a lonely old fellow myself!" Harry gave his deep, rich infectious chuckle. "This is a big city, lass, but I haven't yet met anybody who can drink me under the table."

"But what's happening about your work?" she prompted him, mindful of the cost of the trunk line call.

"Nothing very miraculous," he said cheerfully.

"Is anything wrong, Harry?" She spoke soberly,

knowing Harry's cheerfulness could cover a lot of anguish.

"Nothing, pet, nothing at all. I'll be home Tuesday, so I'll give you all my news then. Where's Pam?"

"She's dressing," she told him quickly. "Nick's here. He's going to take us out to dinner."

"Is he now? You just put him on."

"Do you mean it?" Phone calls cost money.

"Of course," Harry bellowed. "Hang the expense!"

It only took a few seconds to get Nick to the phone and whatever Harry said to him, he burst out laughing.

"Now that, Harry, is ridiculous. Downright slanderous!"

He sounded smooth and amused and a very experienced man of the world.

Kendall could have moved away; instead she hovered in the hallway watching him while he spoke a few moments more on the phone. She shook her head, still a little dazed. She had always thought Nick a very handsome man in a bold, aggressive, very adult kind of way. Now she stared at him objectively with seemingly more perceptive eyes.

As usual he was dressed beautifully, the very best of everything, but now she was struck by his elegance and easy power, his height, the width of his shoulders, the narrow waist and hips, the long legs. Tall, lean men always looked well in their clothes, but surely not so well as Nick? He had good hands, too, beautifully shaped, his gold watch glinting against his darkly tanned skin. In repose, his face was sombre, even intimidating, but now he was smiling at something Harry was saying and his mouth curved in such a way, and you could see his fine white teeth and the way his black eyes lit up. It suddenly struck her what Pamela had seen all along: Nick Langford projected an extraordinary sexuality and now, God help her, she was painfully aware of it.

Nick hung up and turned around to her and she flushed as though he could read her thoughts in her face.

"What's with you?" He reached out and touched her cheek.

"I'm just worrying about Harry," she said evasively.

"Stop worrying. He'll be home Tuesday."

"Did he tell you anything?"

"No, he didn't." Nick looked thoughtful. "It's pretty hard to get Harry to talk sense. On the other hand he talks better nonsense than any other man I know. Don't worry, little one," he looked down into her green, troubled eyes. "Everything will work out."

"Oh, I hope so." She sighed and her fingers reached out and straightened yet another of Harry's paintings with a slight list to port. It was one of her favourites, small, but filled with all the vibrant light of the tropics.

"Harry's good, isn't he, Nick?" she said.

"He has the ability to be a winner." Nick leaned across her shoulder and set the painting unerringly right. In doing so, he touched her fingers and she felt suddenly very weak and helpless.

"Yet somehow he can't seem to get it all together." Her mother had been able to get the best out of Harry, yet somehow it did no good to think about that.

"Here now," Nick turned her to face him, "you're not going to cry?"

"No, I'm *not*!" she said, and her voice trembled. "Have you ever seen me cry?"

"Yes, I have." There was an indulgent note in the deep voice.

"Oh—well, that was years ago." She couldn't look at him, his hands holding her. "I guess I owe you one."

"So why don't you remember more often?"

She still had her head down and he seemed to groan. "Oh God, come on, baby, snap out of it. Not everyone's dream comes true, Kendall, and I'm afraid there's very little you can do about it. The important thing is you love Harry and he surely loves you. In fact, he adores you. If it will make you any happier, I'll speak to him when he comes home.''

"*Will* you?" She lifted her head instantly, her voice a mixture of pleading and relief. Nick was probably the only person they knew Harry took any note of.

"Yes.'' The pressure of his fingers tightened. "Harry's my pal, and I don't like to see you looking wretched.''

He was the same as usual when he was in a good mood, kind, considerate, Big Brother, yet something was different. Kendall looked up at him hungrily as though searching for an answer and he released her abruptly. "Now, aren't you going to follow Pamela's example and change your dress?"

It was plainly withdrawal, yet strangely it settled her. "You don't like what I'm wearing?"

"It's very fetching." He flashed her a bright glance.

"But not good enough for the Golf Club!" She glanced down at herself with a good deal of Harry's cheerfulness. "All right, Nick Langford, you're the boss!''

CHAPTER TWO

HARRY didn't return on Tuesday but wired them to say he was detained on business.

"I suppose he's drinking." Pamela flashed Kendall an angry look across the kitchen table. "He even boasts about it!"

"We don't know that," Kendall choked her coffee down scalding. If she didn't break away now, Pamela would launch into a full-scale recital of her resentments against Harry.

"Oh yes, we do!" Pamela retorted bitterly. "It's always like this, you know, when he goes away alone."

"Don't get yourself all tensed up," Kendall said soothingly. "He's probably met someone who can help him."

Pamela swallowed her orange juice. That was all she had for breakfast, orange juice and black coffee. "How did I every marry him?" she sighed.

"It mustn't have seemed half so bad at the time." Kendall wanted another piece of toast, but she just couldn't risk a scene with her stepmother.

"I suppose you're going?" Pamela's voice sounded as cold and brittle as a piece of ice.

"I'll be late for work if I don't."

"Work!" Pamela gave a contemptuous little shrug of her shoulder. "At your age I was earning big money as a model."

"Too much, maybe. You seem to have spent it."

"Don't give me any flip answers." Pamela's hand began to shake. "I tell you I can't take this any more!"

"I'm sorry." Kendall sat down again, trying hard to be sympathetic. "I suppose you really should get out more. You're a beautiful woman and you've got lots of ability. Why don't you try opening a shop?"

"A *what*?"

"A classy boutique, I suppose." Kendall looked her stepmother over, seeing she would be an excellent self-advertisement.

Even in her bitter state Pamela looked amazed and slightly taken with the idea.

"And what would I do for money?" Under her exquisite peignoir her full breasts rose and fell dramatically. "You know as well as I do, Harry could never finance you. Why, he couldn't even send you on to university."

"I didn't want to go," Kendall lied staunchly. "Maybe the bank would set you up. I'm sure you could make a go of it."

"*You're* sure. I'm *certain*!" Pamela said sharply. "Have you seen those apologies for good dress shops in town?"

"No, not really," Kendall said wryly. Pamela was the only one Harry pampered with a dress allowance. "There's plenty of money around. All the Country Club lot spend hundreds of dollars on a dress as a matter of course."

"But they don't buy in town." A muscle jumped in the side of Pamela's smooth jawline. "In the old days I had tons of friends in the business who could help me."

"Why not look them up again?" Kendall suggested helpfully, glad at least to have diverted Pamela's thoughts.

"They don't lend money, dearie," said Pamela sarcastically. "You know what, I think I'll ask Nick."

"Oh!" Kendall blanked out.

"Why not?" Purpose crept into Pamela's voice. "He has money to burn."

"As a precaution mightn't it be better not to borrow from a friend?"

"I'd say Nick would be pretty safe." Pamela's classic face was unusually animated. "The more I think about it, the better it sounds. Actually you're not too bad with your ideas."

"I'd better fly." Kendall kept her voice friendly. "Wait until Harry gets back and talk it over with him."

Pamela brushed the suggestion off impatiently. "He won't be agreeable, you'll see. All Harry wants is a good companion in bed. He's never seen me as his wife."

"Oh, that's not right!" Kendall stopped dead and stared down at Pamela's ash-blonde head.

"The reason he married me," Pamela continued harshly, "was because I got into his blood. Not his heart and his mind. Those sacred places are filled with the memory of your mother."

"I'm sure that's not right." Kendall looked her distress. "Harry loves you, can't you see that?"

"He loves *you*!" Pamela corrected flatly. "Very briefly he fell in love with me as a model. I'll have to admit it was easy for him to talk me into it. He's charming and virile, but actually he's a bit of a scoundrel."

Kendall shook her glossy head. "Not Harry. He's not as responsible as he should be, I know, but Harry would never do anything dishonest."

"I never meant anything dishonest," said Pamela, "only that he's a diabolical man. Just look at how lazy he's become! I feel like screaming when he just idles away his time. 'It won't work, Pammy,' he says, then throws the brush down and goes off fishing for inspiration."

"At least the fish don't get away." Kendall rested her fingers lightly on Pamela's shoulder. "I promise I'll help you when you speak to him about it. I can see now it's bad for you cooped up all the time at the farmhouse.

You could even open some kind of art shop selling paintings and pottery and what have you.''

"Ugh!'' Pamela vetoed that idea, only interested in a painting if it was one of herself. "Small change. The fashion boutique is the right idea.''

"I'll call you later on in the day. Harry might ring.'' Kendall gathered up her handbag and shopping basket. "Chops do tonight? Or we could manage some fillet steak with my windfall.''

"Strictly speaking it all belongs to Nick.'' Pamela narrowed her eyes. "I mean, he gave you all that silver to play the poker machines.''

"It was just a game. A passing bit of fun. I didn't ask him for anything. He just pulled it all out of his pocket.''

"And helped you pull the lever that provided your windfall.'' Pamela stood up and brushed her hands over her thighs. "I thought it terribly adolescent of you to hug him.''

"He didn't notice in any case. I was so excited.'' Kendall kept her voice light and expressionless though Pamela's bitchy, jealous tone had stabbed her. "Anyway, he was urging me on.''

"Then it's fortunate he's got the Midas touch!'' Pamela gave an explosive, impatient sigh. "Why doesn't Harry come home? Now you've thought this idea up, I want to get on with it.''

ALL MORNING Kendall sat in her small, cluttered office, tossing the idea up herself. It would certainly give Pamela something to do and no doubt she could make a success of it, but she knew she didn't want Pamela to ask Nick to set her up. Harry would be unhappy about it as well. Or would he? Harry often thought differently from herself. Surely a bank or a finance company could help? What had she started with an almost casual remark?

By lunchtime she had a headache. The air-conditioning had broken down and Miss Reed had swooped on the fan. She had shopping to do in town, otherwise she would have stayed at the mill. It was set in very beautiful grounds that sloped away to the river. Although there was an excellent cafeteria, a lot of the employees liked to bring a cut lunch and eat it down by the river. No matter how hot it was, there always seemed to be a breeze and the grounds abounded in magnificent shade trees.

Kendall parked the car at the top end of the main street and walked down the hill. Of course it wasn't going to be so easy going back, but at this time of day central parking was very hard to find. Cars lined both sides of the long, wide street, some very expensive, some dusty and battered, most the ubiquitous station wagons. Langford was a positive, productive coastal town that was fast becoming a city. There were sugar and tea plantations, tropical fruit farms in abundance and a hinterland famous for its livestock. Flamingo Park, pioneered before there had ever been a town, had long enjoyed the reputation for being one of the finest beef cattle stations in the country. There was even a statue of the Hon. John Palmer Langford, Nick's pioneering ancestor, standing in a little island right in the centre of the town. It was even fussed over by the National Heritage Committee, but apparently the Hon. John had been quite a man; a gentleman by birth and breeding but an adventurer by nature with a great lust for expanding his horizons.

Once the Langfords had owned virgin land galore, now the family interests were diversified. Nick had inherited Flamingo Park and a score of family directorships. The Langfords were into everything; Nick and his uncle and cousins who lived in splendid residences on the cliff top overlooking the town and the river. It could be said the Langfords had dominated the whole rich,

fertile valley for as long as anyone could remember.
Harry had once challenged Nick about providing an heir
in case the whole dynasty passed into other than
Langford hands, but Nick had laughed and shook his
head and said he wasn't ready to commit any irrevoc-
able acts, but there was scarcely an eligible female in
the district who wouldn't have fallen apart if he had
looked her way. Even his cousin Thalia. Kendall hated
her and she didn't know why. Thalia was rich and glossy
and even good-looking in a horsey kind of way. What
had possessed her to think she hated her? She didn't
hate anyone. *No!*

Determinedly she did her shopping for the household
and as she came out of the supermarket there was Mrs.
Hogan, and too late now to pretend she hadn't seen her.

"Kendall." Mrs. Hogan's smile was stiff and
restrained.

"How are you, Mrs. Hogan?" Kendall said solemnly.
It seemed the right way to address Colin's mother.

"Not so bad, thank you, dear. How can you race
about so in the heat?"

"I suppose it's my age group."

"Yes." Mrs. Hogan gave her a pitying smile. "Come
and have a cup of tea with me."

Kendall wanted to decline, instead she accepted
gravely. "That would be nice." It just wasn't her day,
with hours yet to go.

Mrs. Hogan ordered tea for two without consulting
Kendall, who loathed it but thought she could drink it at
a pinch. "I'm glad of this opportunity to have a little
chat!" Mrs. Hogan's hat threw a darkness across her
face. "Has your father arrived home yet?"

"No." Kendall didn't feel inclined to elaborate,
knowing full well Mrs. Hogan didn't approve of Harry.
Or Pamela. Or herself, for that matter.

"Just whatever made him decide to buy a farm?"
Mrs. Hogan asked with studied politeness.

"It's a beautiful spot," Kendall pointed out. "We have a marvellous view of the lake and the Lockharts' new tea plantation."

"Ah, yes, the Lockharts." Mrs. Hogan's severe expression lightened miraculously. "It's remarkable how they've been able to rehabilitate themselves. It must have been a blow leaving their property in New Guinea."

"I think they're over it now."

"Sue is a lovely girl, isn't she?" Mrs. Hogan looked unusually enthusiastic.

"Yes, she is." Sue was a very nice girl, sweet and appealing without being at all positive.

The tea arrived and the thin cucumber sandwiches—wholemeal bread—Mrs. Hogan had asked for. "I had hopes for Sue and Colin," Mrs. Hogan said pleasantly, "but then he became entangled with you."

"Entangled?" Kendall looked up, startled.

"He's quite besotted with you, Kendall, and you know it."

"I don't even know what besotted means."

"It means taken up with, enslaved, stupefied," Mrs. Hogan told her in a heavily flat tone. "There doesn't seem to be a day he doesn't mention you."

"In what way?" Kendall was having difficulty keeping her temper. She had always known deep down that Mrs. Hogan disliked her, but she had always been hospitable enough without being friendly. This was different, these cold, accusing eyes. Brown, like Colin's but without the gentle warmth of Colin's expression. It always surprised her how alike yet unalike mother and son were.

"What Kendall thinks—what Kendall likes. He wouldn't even let me put up new curtains without checking with me that Kendall would like them. I ask you, my dear, my *home*!"

"How extraordinary!" Kendall swallowed on the

hasty words that came to her throat. "I like Colin very much, Mrs. Hogan, but there's nothing serious between us."

"Oh, for heaven's sake, grow up!" Mrs. Hogan admonished her. "My son is in love with you. I feel sure he's only waiting for the right moment to ask you to marry him. He's not the farmer his dear father was, but he's learning all the time. Give him another year and I'm sure he'll be ready to settle down."

"But, Mrs. Hogan," Kendall said earnestly. "I don't want to tie myself down to the responsibilities of marriage for a long time."

"Of course," Mrs. Hogan drank her tea pleasurably, "you've had a very unsettled upbringing."

"That sounds vaguely insulting!" Kendall's emerald green eyes began to flash fire.

"It wasn't meant to be!" The older woman drew in her lip in reproval. "I've said before today, Kendall, you're far too aggressive. You see insults where they're never intended. It doesn't lead me to believe you'd make a good wife for Colin."

"No, I'll admit it!" Kendall folded her paper napkin.

"Please don't go!" Belatedly Mrs. Hogan got wind of her intention. "Colin would never forgive me if I upset you. The thing is, Kendall, I want the best for my boy. You will one day too, when you have a son. I know you both enjoy being together and I can see you're a very pretty girl, but it seems to me you don't really care about Colin, not in the way he cares about you. It may be that you're too young, you said yourself you're not ready to assume responsibility, but I don't want you wasting his time. If you don't want him, let him go. Believe me, I'll stand by him and pick up the pieces."

"I don't think that will be necessary, Mrs. Hogan," Kendall said crisply. "I've never given Colin any cause to fall apart."

"See, it's that flippancy in you!" Mrs. Hogan's thin

face looked agitated. "Can't you understand, Kendall, why I had to talk to you?"

"Not really, no." She hadn't even touched her tea, though no doubt it would have helped her now pounding headache. "Colin can surely handle his own life. We're good friends and I value his friendship, but I have no designs on him at all."

"I could like you better if you did!" A flush rose to the older woman's cheeks, but she didn't raise her quiet voice by a decibel. "They say girls with green eyes are heartless."

"Of course there are historical reasons," Kendall entered into the lunacy of it. "Witches and so forth." She stood up a little hastily so Mrs. Hogan had to steady her teacup. "Please forgive me, but I must fly."

"Wait, Kendall!" Mrs. Hogan looked upset, and just as suddenly Kendall's kind heart smote her.

"No, really, I'll be late." She made an effort to smile. "Perhaps it's the way you're feeling that's making you get things a little out of perspective. If so, I understand, and I promise you I'll never hurt Colin. I like him too much."

Just how well *do* I like him? she thought to herself as she raced madly uphill. Mrs. Hogan was surely exaggerating Colin's emotions. She had seen very little evidence of a strong passion herself, yet Nick, too, with his hard, level gaze, had told her Colin was in love with her. Did this mean she had to give him up? Miss out on an uncomplicated boy-girl relationship? Perhaps Mrs. Hogan had a point. Was she being selfish? Using Colin for her own ends? He played a pretty good game of tennis, not *too* good so she was hopelessly outclassed, and he had taught her how to ride a surfboard. Some passion!

By the time she reached the car her heart was knocking against her ribs. Her shopping bag seemed dreadfully heavy and she had difficulty finding her key. When she finally switched on the ignition, the engine didn't fire as usual, but gave a sick croak and petered out. Kendall swore mildly under her breath and tried again. Three croaks this time. The next time, just nothing. A flat battery.

It eased her a little to bash the wheel, then she thought she had better get out and ring work. Another phone call wouldn't endear her to Miss Reed, the VW had broken down before, but there was nothing else for it. She had the meat, as well, eye fillet for Pamela, and it would take that much longer to get it into a fridge.

By the time she made it down to the phone box, she felt almost ready to drop. Even eighteen-year-olds couldn't rush around in the heat. Of course she didn't have ten cents and just as she considered shrieking on the sidewalk, a long powerful car drew up beside her. It was Nick.

Frantically, she opened the door on the passenger side and slid in. "My hero!"

"What the hell have you been doing?" His black eyes flashed over her pale face and the damp curls that were forming all over her head. "You look as if you're about to flake out."

"Oh, I *am*!" She fell back against the rich leather, revelling in the wonderful airconditioning. "First of all I had a cosy chat with Mrs. Hogan, and as if that wasn't enough I couldn't get the car to start."

"Where is it?" Nick turned her face to him, frowning at the pallor under her golden tan.

"Up the hill."

"And you've been racing up and down?"

"Saves dieting. Wouldn't that be terrible!"

"Be quiet and relax." He spoke like a doctor, quiet-toned and no-nonsense.

"Gosh!" She shut her eyes. "Can you lend me ten cents, I have to ring work."

"Will you stop acting like a strung-up child!" He pushed her back into the seat. "I'll ring for you."

"Miss Reed," she called to him. "Ask for Miss Reed." The old dragon—most of the staff were agreed on that.

Inexplicably her legs were trembling and she felt quite giddy. Perhaps she was in shock. Let Nick handle it; he knew everyone and everyone knew him.

When he got back into the car again she had her eyes firmly closed to stop the world spinning.

"Do you feel faint?" he demanded.

"Just a little."

"You're supposed to put your head down, not back." He grasped her by the nape and tipped her head forward so it was almost in her lap.

After a minute she began to feel better. "Did you get on to Miss Reed?"

"Hang Miss Reed!" He still had his hand on her nape.

"Some of us would like to." Kendall brought her head up and her hair tumbled in a silky black cloud all about her face. "What did she say?"

"I didn't speak to her, actually," he said finally. "I spoke to Bob Stirling."

"The boss?" she exclaimed.

"Probably Miss Reed wouldn't have taken much heed of me. You're having the afternoon off."

"What exactly did you say?" It took an awful effort to keep the wobble out of her voice.

"As I see it, I don't have to tell you." He looked at her critically, seeing the colour come back into her face. "You know, Kendall, sometimes you tear me up."

"Make you angry?" She turned her head sideways, sounding helpless and a little vague.

"That too." His brilliant eyes pinioned her. "Where's this cute little car of yours?"

"Right up the top of Lake St. It won't go. I've tried."

For once she didn't resent his masterfulness, but settled back tiredly like a spent child. When they pulled ahead of her car she handed him the keys, let him satisfy himself it was a flat battery, then return to his own perfect example of modern engineering.

"A flat battery!" He gave her a charming, sardonic look.

"I figured that myself. Sometimes machines are so boring."

"What did Mrs. Hogan have to say to you?" asked Nick.

"It was more in the nature of an ultimatum."

"So that's why you're so upset?"

"I'm not!—and where are you taking me?"

"Where do you want to go?" His eyes touched the satiny skin of her arched throat.

"Home." She didn't, but some vestige of sanity clung to her. "Harry sent us a telegram. He's been delayed on business."

"Oh?" He sounded hard and unconvinced.

"Damn you, Nick!" She said it softly, weakly.

"And damn you, green eyes."

HARRY CAME HOME on the Friday and that very evening he and Pamela had a flaming row.

"You've never kept a single promise you made me!" Pamela's normally matt white skin was flushed rosy.

"For God's sake, what's so terrible about that?" Harry said defensively. "Just how many men keep their promises?"

"You cad!" Pamela rushed to the bed, picked up Harry's pillow and threw it out the door like an avenging angel. "Get out!"

"And how am I supposed to take *that*?" Harry shouted, a pirate of a man with a golden head and beard and vivid, sun-creased blue eyes.

"An expression of protest!" Pamela plunged to the

door and held it ready to slam. "You're ruining yourself, Harry, drinking and neglecting your work. Just
how long do you think I'm going to sit around watching
you drink whisky for breakfast? Why, you haven't done
any real work in ages—Rudy told you."

Harry laughed acidly. "And didn't you tell *him*!
Reviled him so he had to race for the door."

"Who cares? I never liked him, the little weasel!"
Pamela shrieked in disgust. "You're like all men, thinking you can get away with anything, but I tell you, I've
had it!"

"Now, Pammy—!" Harry began doubtfully.

"Don't Pammy me, you great oaf!" She slammed the
door so powerfully, Kendall taking refuge in the kitchen
speculated on how long it would take for the iron roof
to cave in.

"Phew!" Harry came to the kitchen door and tried a
sheepish grin. "Would you mind telling me what
brought *that* on?"

"Serves you right, Harry," Kendall said with strict
fairness.

"Ah, a traitor in our midst!" Harry shifted un-
comfortably and sat down at the table. "Be a good girl
and get me a drink."

"No."

"Just one. I'm needing it."

"It's too easy for you, this bending the elbow," said
Kendall crossly.

"I tell you I'm fed up!" Harry's fine, fair skin was
unusually blotchy.

"You're all right, aren't you?" She touched his arm
in sudden alarm. "There's a lot of red under your
skin."

"No doubt it's my blood pressure," he joked. "Can't
you get me that drink, darling? For your poor old
father?"

"Oh, Harry!" She stood up and leaned over him,

linking her arms about his neck and kissing the top of his springy golden head. "No wonder some people find the wicked booze horrifying. You aren't in pain or anything?"

"*No!*" he hastened to reassure her. "I'm as strong as an ox—make that oaf."

"If you ask me you're not!" Kendall said forlornly. "If you think you've got high blood pressure, it has to be treated. You've got to be sensible, Harry. Your life is at stake."

"Show me the way to the cemetery!"

"It's not a joke. It's deadly serious!" Kendall scolded him.

"Now don't you start minding my business," Harry warned her. "One impossible woman in the house is enough."

"You brought it all on yourself tonight."

"No doubt about that!" He gave a harsh, rumbling laugh. "I plead guilty. Now can I please have that drink?"

"If you must," she sighed deeply. "I suppose it will calm you."

"It does every time."

Kendall clicked her tongue and walked into the living room, going to the expensive bar in the corner. Such a terrible waste of money when so many other things could have been done with it. She poured a disgracefully small whisky, splashed water into it and went back to her father.

"That's it!" she said firmly.

"Thank you, darling!" Harry took the tumbler from her, then muttered in disgust. "Surely you don't call *that* a whisky?"

"Many people would."

Harry breathed gustily. "For God's sake think carefully before you ever get married."

"I'll think carefully before I ever get *engaged*!" Kendall resumed her chair, staring into Harry's face. "We've never spoken of this, Harry, but you love Pamela, don't you?"

"A...a...ah!" Harry drew out a sigh.

"Please tell me. I know Pamela's unhappy."

"But, my little darling, that's perfectly normal for Pamela." Harry drained off his drink like an explorer in the desert. "To tell the truth, darling, I don't."

"Oh, Harry!" Kendall felt real distress for Pamela.

"Shock you, does it?" Harry stared in concentration at the kitchen sink. "For a few breathless weeks there I thought I was in love with her, or the person I invented, but there's very little to Pamela, as you know. In fact, you've been an angel of understanding."

"Yet she deserves more than you're giving her," Kendall said sadly.

"Would you say that *I* don't?" Harry shifted his gaze to look at her and she saw a great loneliness.

"Oh, Daddy!" All the tears she had held back over the years suddenly sprang to her eyes and poured down her cheeks.

"Don't cry, darling!" Harry reached out roughly and stroked her hair. "God knows these arguments are beyond all endurance."

"It's *you*!" she quavered, his expression indelibly etched on her mind.

"I was lost a long time ago—five years, to be exact. Every day of my life I mourn her. My life began and ended with your mother. Now I'm living in some no-man's-land with everything vital missing, no purpose, no landmarks, no direction. Why do you think I didn't let you go away to university? Because I needed you here desperately, that's why. I know, I'm selfish. I know, I know. Pamela and I are just a masquerade.

"How dreadful!" Kendall lifted her tear-streaked face. "She cares a good deal more for you than you think."

"Ah well," Harry shrugged his heavy shoulders, "when it comes to it I care about her too, but it's not love, darling. Not like I loved my Rachel. Life plays some dreadful games with us and we're not permitted an appeal. I lost my wife and you lost your mother."

"But, Harry, you took on the responsibility of Pamela," Kendall told him earnestly, dashing the tears from her cheeks. "You can't just give up on her, or yourself. God, Harry, you're only fifty!"

"Forty-eight!" Harry flashed back, outraged. "Don't you go around telling people how old I am!"

"I *don't*!" she maintained with considerable severity. Harry always lied about his age. "I don't know whether you actually believe this, but you have it in your power to make yourself and Pamela a whole lot happier than you are."

"She's doing fine," Harry said shortly.

"No, she's not. I'm telling you she knows she's second best, and that must be a dreadful way to feel. You can change all that, Harry. You're the best actor I know and after a while you'll grow right into the role. You're not *trying*."

"That's just the point," he said with black humour. "I have to *try*. Over and over and over."

"Doesn't everyone?" Kendall was dismayed at his attitude. "You and Mummy used to have arguments."

"And after they were over...." Harry's blue eyes clouded over in remembrance. "Rachell was all spirit and fire, but inside of her there was such peace. The only real peace I've ever known. You're too young to know what real love is about. I had it with Rachel and she spoilt me for anyone else."

"Stop it, Harry!" She shook him fiercely. "Maybe you'd better start thinking about how other people feel rather than yourself."

"Hey now!" He looked down into her vivid face, shocked.

"I suffered too, Harry," she told him. "You're not the only one mourning Mamma."

"My darling!" Harry peered into the brilliant green eyes. "Forgive me."

"Naturally, I always do." Kendall stood up tiredly, a small slender girl who could look hauntingly lovely. "I'd better make up your bed in the guest room."

"Familiar territory!" Harry cried. "Why the hell does she always throw the pillow out? I can't figure that one out."

"You could try and make your peace."

"Certainly I could," Harry agreed suavely, "but she's probably shut down for the night."

"Poor Pamela!" sighed Kendall.

In the spare room, she made up the bed with the ease of long practice while Harry sat in the armchair looking as if he was contemplating the various ways to commit suicide.

"I'll hunt up some pyjamas for you," she said bracingly.

"Don't bother."

"Certainly I will. What if we had a visit from the fire brigade?"

Harry grunted in acknowledgment. "Or the nuns."

"Now, Harry—"

"There's Forsyth," he suddenly volunteered. "He's agreed to take three or four of my big canvases."

"Great!" Kendall's small oval face brightened into radiance. "Why didn't you say so before?"

"I haven't painted them yet," he said sourly.

"Maybe you haven't heard the old saying: a journey of a thousand miles begins with the first step."

Harry nodded. "That's the trouble. It's mostly uphill."

"Never mind." She threw his pyjamas at him. "You're a big, strong six-footer."

"So I am. A Viking, if I say so myself."

"Harry!" she knelt down in front of him and looked into his eyes, "I was thinking—"

"Not again!"

"About a way we could all get rich."

"Would it have anything to do with Nick?" Harry demanded with an effortful control of his voice.

"Nick?" Kendall repeated the name with a look of astonishment. "Has Pamela spoken to you?"

"Pamela? What is this all about?"

"A job for Pamela," she said compellingly, her green eyes burning in her golden face. "She needs some outside interest, some challenge. Preferably something that will make money. You're a great believer in women working. Encourage her to get a job. I think she'd be excellent at running a dress boutique."

"My dearest child!" Harry gave her such a pitying look one would have thought she had taken leave of her senses. "Can you really see Pamela *working*? For another *woman*? Or even dealing with them. It can't have skipped your attention that she's never learned the gentle art of diplomacy. My dear, she'd loathe it. She'd assault somebody. She's a very vain person. She has to be the centre of attention."

"She could be, with her own shop!" Kendall argued with the air of a magician pulling a rabbit out of his hat.

"Your next enterprise, please." Harry's eyes sparkled with sardonic humour. "One needs capital to start a business, pretty one. Oh, my God," he suddenly sobered and struck his right temple, "she's not thinking of asking Nick?"

"No, not at all!" Kendall lied easily in a good cause, "but there's nothing wrong with asking his advice. I mean, Nick's the resident financial wizard. I'm sure he'd be happy to assess the whole situation. Pamela has a great flair and if she was running the show she could turn on the charm."

"She's not in that business tonight," Harry returned

acidly, and thumped the pillow. "Let me sleep on it, darling," he said dismissively. "Not everyone has your courage and confidence."

"But it's not a bad idea, is it?"

"Actually it's not." Harry chewed his golden moustache. "I may just give of my own talents. I'd be a splendid marketing man and I could even whip up a few designs in my spare time."

"So we'll speak to Nick tomorrow night?"

"Not about capital," Harry frowned formidably. "Nick has too many people trying to put the bite on him. I want his friendship more than any other I know. I won't have it spoilt by introducing the sordid topic of money."

"My thoughts exactly!" Kendall threw her arms around her father and hugged him. He had taken it all so well. Now all she had to do was speak to Nick.

A GOOD NIGHT'S SLEEP worked wonders for Harry and next morning both women woke to the delicious aromas of perking coffee and grilled bacon wafting from the kitchen.

Kendall arrived first, knowing full well it couldn't possibly be Pamela unless she had undergone a tremendous temperamental upheaval.

"Morning, darling," Harry called, looking the picture of perfect health.

"Well, well, this is a surprise!" She looked with delight at the fresh tablecloth, the neatly arranged table and a little spray of the beautiful Malaya Summer arranged like strawberry icecream in a vase centre table.

"All in a day's work!" Harry poured pineapple juice into three tall frosted glasses. "Would your dear stepmamma be about?"

"Better make that orange juice for Pamela," Kendall suggested. "I think the pineapple gives her an acid stomach."

Harry laughed. "Orange juice it is. I aim to please."

Kendall picked up her pineapple juice and drank it down. "You look as though you slept well," she told him.

"Actually I lay in the dark for hours thinking about your idea."

"Then it must have your approval." The juice was so refreshing Kendall drank the glassful Harry had poured for Pamela.

"Well, let's just say it gave me pause." Harry efficiently ladled bacon and eggs on to two plates. "See if Pam's up, will you, darling. You know, break the ice."

"No need to." Pamela came to the kitchen door with her face free of make-up and her long blonde hair tucked into a roll. "I have to hand it to you, Harry, when you think you think big!"

"Thank you, darling. There are many sides to me, but I rarely use them." He put the frying pan down and came around the table, curling an arm around Pamela's waist and kissing her full on the mouth. "This is an apology for last night."

"And I'm grateful. . . so grateful!" Pamela was torn between sincerity and sarcasm.

"Go on, you missed me, you know you did."

"Stop playing games, Harry!" Flushed and cajoled, Pamela looked a good ten years younger.

"Look, dearest, my motives are as clear as glass. I'm trying to say I'm sorry. You're too good for me, that's what you are." He swung her closer to him and gave her another grunting kiss. "What's this I hear about your wanting to play shop?"

"Why not?" Pamela looked quickly at Kendall, who nodded.

"I spoke to Harry last night. So far he's enthusiastic."

"Sit down, girls. If you're not careful everything will

go cold." Harry held the chair for Pamela who took it eagerly and winked over her blonde head at Kendall. "You can tell me all about it over a long, leisurely breakfast."

"In that case, I think I'll have the works!" For once Pamela was moved to forget her stringent diet.

"Here, have mine." Kendall placed her plate in front of her stepmother. "Harry, sit down and have yours. It will only take me a minute to make more."

It took them more than an hour to talk the whole subject over and it was unanimously agreed they should seek Nick's advice. Nick was the expert in money matters and legal requirements, and as Pamela seemed to fit the role she proposed to take up and the opportunity was there, he could even be moved to assist. That was Pamela's view, but Harry pointed out that banks and finance institutions existed for just that purpose.

Animation lent Pamela's somewhat expressionless face an added interest. "I could even, if it came to that, have clothes made up to my own design. Or we could do it together, Harry. Remember that evening dress you designed for me? You have quite an eye for women's fashions and you're an excellent draughtsman."

"What?" Harry poured mock scorn into the suggestion. "Demean myself designing women's dresses?"

"You wouldn't exactly loathe being rich," she told him dryly. "Think of all the bottles of whisky you could bring home."

"Now, now, *I'm* trying." Harry looked at his wife for two seconds and she flushed.

"Sorry, darling." She put a hand on his arm. "The thing is, if we're going to impress Nick and everyone else at that party, we'll need to buy Kendall a new dress. You and I generally turn heads, but she doesn't even possess one decent dress for the evening."

"There's nothing new in not painting the lily," Harry glanced at his beautiful young daughter. "But I take your meaning. How do you propose to rustle up something ravishing at this late hour?''

"We'll just have to go into town." Pamela narrowed expert eyes over Kendall's slender figure. "Of course we won't get what I want, but she's young enough and slim enough to get away with anything."

Set on her venture, Pamela dragged Kendall through the few dress shops she deemed fit to be seen in, and just when Kendall had just about had enough, they found it: a little bit of nothing that looked terrific on. It looked so good even Kendall was excited, though it was much more sophisticated and figure-revealing than any dress she ever wore. Showing the curves of her breasts was one thing on the beach, but quite another rising from a black silk camisole dipped in gold and crimson.

"You'll do!" said Pamela with approval, and didn't even flinch as she passed over the money. "At least that snooty bitch Thalia Langford won't be able to look down her long nose at us."

"Be nice to her," Kendall warned with a smile, "you just could have her for a customer!"

CHAPTER THREE

By the time they arrived at the party, nearly everyone had arrived. There were cars everywhere along the great curving driveway; not a practical four-cylinder job in sight, but cars of distinction; Mercedes aplenty, a Daimler, a Porsche, a couple of Ferraris, Cadillacs, a distressingly red Pontiac Firebird and Noel Langford's navy blue Rolls.

"The filthy rich!" Harry said cheerfully, "but I hold no dreadful grudge against them."

However, Kendall noticed, he avoided the lot of them, and parked their rather primitive but reliable old Holden a discreet distance away.

"So what do we do now," Pamela asked crossly, "take a taxi?"

"You have a very poor opinion of your legs," Harry said lightly. "They should hold you up until you reach the front door."

"It's my *hair* I'm talking about!" Pamela cried, sincerely concerned that the breeze would disarrange her impeccable coiffure and turn Kendall's face framing style into a gypsy riot.

"Why don't you drop us both outside, Harry," Kendall suggested. "We'll wait for you at the stairs."

"All right, then," Harry sighed gustily. "Women worry about such bloody silly things!"

Her anxieties alleviated, Pamela leaned forward to take in the view. "Isn't this the most incredible place?" she raved.

"I wouldn't mind owning it," Harry said gruffly.

The house was ablaze with lights and the extensive grounds were floodlit on all sides. "It would cost a few million to build it these days, even if there were the craftsmen around."

"What style would you call it, Harry?" Kendall, too, was excited and impressed.

"Baronial!" Harry said instantly. "Memories of home. It must cost a fortune to maintain."

"Ah well, Nick's got it," Pamela murmured complacently. "It's so wonderfully sited, sitting on the crest of the hill. I've always loved those white columns. They're so romantic, aren't they? Like the deep South. It must be splendid to be rich."

"I could bear it!" Harry's voice was dry. He brought the car to a halt at the base of the low, wide steps.

"We'll wait for you here," Kendall told him, and got out.

"Right." Harry set the car jerkily in motion again.

"Why the devil we can't afford a new car, I'll never know!" Pamela said fretfully.

"Never mind, if things go according to plan, you'll be able to get yourself a Rolls like the Langfords."

"I'll fix that in mind."

They ascended two of the steps and stood in the shadow of one of the great white marble lions that stood guard at either side of the steps.

"There's a story about these lions," Kendall said, and patted a cool, inanimate mane. "How they were brought hundreds of miles from the port by bullock waggons. They're carved out of the finest white Italian marble."

"Really?" Pamela wasn't interested in the lions at all. "Where's Harry?" she groaned. "Oh, there he is now." Harry's tall, heavy-shouldered figure appeared out of the trees.

"Further away this time," he grumbled. "Some other blighter took my spot. No sign of him, though."

"Let's go up." Pamela was anxious to make her entrance. Tonight she looked like an imperial Roman goddess, all in white, with a gold rope loosely tying her tunic. Her make-up was superb and she looked every spectacular inch the great model she once had been.

Harry looked her over with complete approval and the hard, critical gaze of the artist, but when he turned his tawny head to look at his daughter, his expression softened like magic. Although Kendall had told them she felt strange in her expensive new dress, she looked a vision of innocent young seductiveness—and so beautifully finished. Trust Pamela to take care of that, even if her motives were almost entirely selfish. She had even supervised Harry's dressing, much to his irritation, but there was no doubt about it, when they were all turned out, they looked a handsome trio.

Nick was on hand to greet them, the elegance of his clothes accentuating the lean strength of his body. He looked suave and handsome and very much one with his grand surroundings.

Pamela blossomed and Harry beamed while Kendall stood there a little hesitantly, feeling in the first instant overawed, even frightened.

"I can't even think this is the same little Kendall," Nick murmured for her alone.

There were people everywhere, spilling out of the two huge reception rooms into the spacious entrance hall. Several called a greeting to Harry and Pamela, then she was left alone with Nick. This was the first big party of Nick's she had ever attended, for he moved in circles vastly different from her own. It was different for Harry and Pamela. They were confident, mature people: Pamela through her physical beauty, which alone set her apart, Harry through his gift and his own witty, entertaining personality. Kendall was eighteen years old and feeling it.

Nick was still holding on to her hand, his thumb

pressing down on her palm. "What are you so nervous of?"

"Mixing with all these beautiful people."

"You'll do fine." His coal-black eyes rested on her hair, the gold-sheened skin of her face, her bare shoulders and the slight swell of her breasts. "Just fine."

A tall, pencil-slim figure in scarlet jersey with slit sides, cut her way through the crowd. "Ah, there you are, Nick!" The brilliant smile faded a little ludicrously as her dark gaze took in the slender girl at his side. "Why, it's...it's..." she searched purposely, in vain.

"Kendall Reardon," Nick supplied dryly. "This is my cousin Thalia, Kendall."

"But, my dear, I scarcely knew you!" Thalia was now holding Nick's elbow, lightly but possessively. "You're all grown up!"

"You're not the only one to notice," Nick murmured sardonically. Quite a few eligible males were hovering on their perimeter, their bright gazes fixed with interest on Kendall. "Ah well, let's get it over," Nick shrugged. "If any one of them starts to bother you, Kendall, you're to come and tell me at once."

"*Bother* her?" Thalia threw him a dark, astonished glance. "Surely she's old enough to look after herself?"

"No, she's not," he said firmly, "and I'm a very responsible host."

From then on, Kendall found herself circulating constantly. She knew a lot of people by sight, so it wasn't difficult to remember names, nor hold the interest of the young men who tired to monopolise her. Harry was holding court at the far end of the huge, beautiful drawing room, Pamela enthroned like a queen at his side, and it was nice to know she didn't have to rely on them for support.

The young men who drove very expensive cars, she found, weren't so very different from the young men of her own circle. They were better dressed, of course. Maybe their vowel sounds were a bit more polished, and they all possessed a certain careless arrogance, but she found she could handle them just as easily. They could even bore her as well, with their exaggerated compliments and the way their eyes watched her mouth while she talked.

One of them, older and more determined than the rest, scooped her up and carried her off to the rear terrace; an enormous, informal entertainment area, where groups of people were sitting around laughing and talking or watching the disco dancers gyrating in a wide semi-circle in front of them.

"I just love her, don't you?" Her partner—his name was Dean Hallitt—swung her expertly into the throng.

"Who?" Automatically her body began to move rhythmically.

"Donna Summer." Dean's light eyes were moving with obvious approval over Kendall's self-assured movements. She was a born dancer, light, graceful, with a pronounced sense of rhythm.

"Oh yes." She smiled at him, wishing he wasn't concentrating on her so intently. It was rather disconcerting. She didn't really like close-set eyes, though many women would have called him good-looking.

"Who taught you to move?" He spun her away from him and back again.

"You're pretty good yourself." It was true.

"Good enough when I've got a partner like you. If you let yourself go a bit more, you'd be sensational."

It took quite a few moments for her to realise the other couples were moving away from them, giving them more room to move.

"Looks like we're on show!" Dean told her, not at all loath to be the centre of attention. "Come on, sweetie, give it all you've got!"

Someone turned the music up, so the night was filled

with the hot, pagan rhythm, then the laughing crowd of
onlookers began to clap, putting their hands together to
intensify the up-tempo beat.

It was like being on some kind of high. Dean wasn't
smiling at all, but as serious as you like, really concentrating on what he was doing. Kendall had to match
him, for she had the feeling he was the kind of man who
turned bitchy when something didn't suit him.

Had she only known it, she was more than matching
him; moving quicker and neater with more originality,
her flying skirt showing the full length of her beautifully
slender legs.

When the music stopped, she wanted to escape the
loud burst of applause. Most of all she wanted to escape
Dean, for he pulled her into his arms and kissed her full
on her parted mouth. She didn't like it at all; his ef-
frontery and the kiss. It was hot and damp and quite
shockingly intimate.

It took a full minute for her vision to clear, then instantly she saw Nick. Unlike everyone else, he wasn't
smiling at all, though there was no denying he was utter-
ly absorbed in them.

"Now that was some experience!" Dean still had her
firmly by the arm. "You're terrific—and I do mean
that!"

"Now I need to sit down." Her voice sounded nervous.

As they moved nearer the sea of tables and Dean
accepted the wealth of compliments, Thalia, who
was standing with Nick, called out to them challengingly:

"That was some performance!"

"How long were you watching?" Dean, who apparently knew her well, smiled a little maliciously.

"Right from the beginning." From her superior
height she glanced down into Kendall's flushed face.
"You could easily be a professional, dear." She spoke

lightly, laughingly, yet it had an undertone Kendall didn't care for.

"It's all about rhythm," Dean told Thalia rather pointedly. "Now you, dear, are absolutely perfect on a horse, but on the dance floor...."

"I'm sure she'd improve out of sight with a little expert guidance." Nick spoke for the first time. "Why not give her a lesson now?"

"I'm not sure I want one!" Thalia brushed the suggestion off impatiently.

"Why not try?" Nick said pleasantly, and reached out and grasped Kendall by the arm. "This child looks as if she needs some refreshment."

Dean pursed his thin mouth. "Looks like we're not wanted, darling!" He grinned tightly at Thalia. "Come along. There should be some simple steps you can master."

With her head thrown back and looking decidedly offended, Thalia followed Dean on to the floor.

"Didn't take you long, did it?" Nick murmured to Kendall without looking at her.

"I don't know what you mean." Her eyes looked enormous, a little vague and unfocused.

"Then I'll spell it out for you. Don't go getting tangled with yet another inadequate type. Dean Hallitt is a lot more dangerous than anyone you're used to."

For a moment she held her breath like a child in shock, then she burst out wrathfully. "You must be mad!"

"Not in front of an audience, little one." He put his hand beneath her elbow and guided her further away towards the floodlit pool, sparkling like an iridescent turquoise jewel. "No, I'm not mad," he continued crisply. "I don't want you associating at all with Hallitt. Understand me?"

Bewildered, Kendall looked up at him, seeing the relentless set to his cleft chin. "But I've only just met him tonight. In *your* house."

"And already he's had the infernal hide to kiss your open mouth."

"I hated it!" she shuddered.

"*I* failed to notice that," he said curtly. "And I'm damned sure he didn't notice either. Steer clear of him, Kendall. He's not suitable company for a young girl."

The deliberate command in his words shocked and startled her. "Damn you, Nick," she said angrily, "you can't talk to me like that!"

"Oh yes, I can!" His own anger flowed to her, absorbing her own. "I'm sorry I asked him."

"Why *did* you?" She had to throw back her head, he was so tall.

"I do a lot of business with his father," he said coolly.

"So he's useful!"

"In a way. What the hell!" He broke off impatiently. "He and Thalia came close to getting engaged once."

"How delightful!" She was trembling now. "I hadn't heard. We move in such different circles, you know."

"Don't go all temperamental on me," he warned her.

"Could it be because you're insulting me?" Her luminous eyes flashed.

"If I am, I'm sorry. Better I insult you than anyone else."

"And to think I was enjoying myself!" Her young voice sounded stormy.

"Little girls need rescuing from predators," said Nick more evenly, his anger dying down. "There are others here you can enjoy yourself with."

"Not *you*!" she snapped. "Oh—Nick!" as he grasped her bare shoulders, hurting her.

"Sorry, but I don't think you know quite when to stop."

If he hadn't held her prisoner she would have risked

making a spectacle of herself and run away across the grass. As it was, she had to stand there. "Don't you have to circulate?" she asked him, her voice brittle as if she was on the brink of tears.

"It wouldn't be you, if you didn't overdo it."

"So what are you so angry about? One stupid kiss?"

"*Sick!* It was sick all the way. I could have smashed him to the ground. I still might."

"Nick!" Her voice shook slightly. "Please stop. I don't think I can stay if you're angry with me."

"Then I'll have to change." His mouth twisted in self-derision. "Relax now—I will. But understand about Hallitt. You had to be warned."

From then on, no matter what she was doing, or who she was talking to, if she turned her head, Kendall encountered Nick's lancing glance. It couldn't have been plainer that he was keeping his eye on her, just as it was apparent her father and stepmother weren't. Harry was in a characteristic gregarious mood, keeping everyone around him in gales of laughter, all the while drinking steadily, while Pamela, for a wonder, was making a real effort to be pleasant to all the older ladies. Normally, and she would have been the first one to admit it, she found the company of her own sex an utter waste of time, but tonight her sights were set differently. These were all moneyed, influential women. Women who could be persuaded to patronise a first-class boutique. She knew for a fact none of them shopped in town when it came to something special, so the market was there.

An hour later, maybe more, Dean Hallitt, like a stalking tiger, caught up with his prey. Kendall had done her level best to keep out of his territory and it wasn't all that difficult. Inner agitation had lent her an extra fire and she was starting to learn her own power. As Nick had told her, there were plenty of others to enjoy herself with.

The very first minute, however, that she found herself

alone, Dean elbowed his way to her side and she noticed how cruel his mouth was under his trendy black moustache.

"You've been avoiding me, haven't you, love?" he asked insolently.

"Why, not at all!" She feigned wide-eyed surprise.

"I suppose Nick dropped a few private words in your pretty ear."

"Really he said nothing at all."

"You're not a very good liar, are you?" he told her drawlingly. "He's even looking daggers at us now. Arrogant devil, Nick—rich, handsome, compelling, ruthless when he has to be, a man of power and influence. My dear old dad is always comparing me unfavourably with him. What's his interest in you?"

"That of a good host, I imagine." Kendall told the truth as she saw it.

"Come off it!" he jeered crudely. "You're a very beautiful girl, or haven't you found that out yet?"

He half turned his body so that she was trapped against the edge of a large sofa and a magnificent Coromandel screen. His eyes were very pale, an almost transparent grey, and they pinned her as effectively as the gorgeous butterflies on the lacquered screen behind her.

"By the way," he said confidingly, "did you know you were putting dear Thalia's long nose out of joint?"

"How is that?" Kendall found her voice in a rush of anger.

"She doesn't like the way Nick has taken you under his wing. Thalia would dearly love to be there, you know."

"Surely not? They're cousins."

"Now you're a sensible girl," he guffawed, "but Thalia isn't. She's been madly in love with Nick since we were all kids together. Incestuous, I call it."

"Oh, really!" He was beginning to disgust her.

"Surely I heard you were nearly engaged to her yourself?"

His mouth stretched in a mirthless smile. "Don't feel sorry for me, dolly. I was never in love with dear old Thalia, only her connections."

With relief Kendall saw the young man who had gone off to get her a drink moving back towards her.

"Here, Dave!" she lifted her hand.

His ugly-attractive freckled face lit up and Dean smiled sourly. "Dave Masterson, what a bore!"

"I like him."

Mercifully he didn't bother her again, and Kendall went in to supper with Dave and his twin brother. Neither of them posed a threat to her peace of mind and she found herself restored to a spurious gaiety. The food was sumptuous, but she didn't feel in the least hungry. All this playing games! Now the warning Thalia Langford was feeling hurt and resentful. She surely didn't understand.

After the prolonged supper, all the frenzy of disco gave way to a lot dreamier, less energetic style of dancing. Kendall had seen Pamela in the powder room when they both went to repair their make-up and Pamela had told her there simply hadn't been the opportunity to talk any kind of business with Nick. Maybe she could broach the subject herself, if she saw him alone. Apparently Pamela thought her good at getting Nick's ear. Another sad misconception!

Feeling like a puppet to be manipulated, she walked with a bent head out on to the softly lit terrace and almost into Nick's arms.

"Hey there!"

Kendall threw up her head, startled, watching his eyes change as he realised who he held. Oh, damn him! For the second time that evening she wanted to run away.

"Sorry, I wasn't looking where I was going," she apologised.

"It's all right. I was looking for you in any case."

"Oh—why?"

"Don't stay mad at me, little one!"

She shook her head, feeling a crazy mixture of feelings that stretched her nerves taut. Everywhere around her everyone was so bright and alive. There were even people in the pool now, diving and splashing and calling to others to come in.

"You're not tired, are you?" He tilted her chin. "I think you've been paid a bit too much attention."

"Well, I certainly didn't ask for it," she said tartly.

"Come here." Nick hauled her very gently into his arms, allowing her to cling to him under the guise of dancing.

She must have craved it, the softening in him, the physical contact, for her whole body yielded. "You're a brute, Nick!"

"But, baby, somebody has to look out for you." His hand moved almost caressingly over her back.

"Are you sure you haven't got it all on video-tape?"

"I'll admit it. I was watching you—yes."

A strange excitement was spreading right through her body, like a dangerous drug. She had to make an effort to regain her poise.

"This is a glorious house," she said sincerely.

"You haven't seen half of it. I'll show you if you so desire."

"How many bedrooms?" She was saying anything that came into her head.

"That's an interesting question, Kendall!" He glanced down at her and there was laughter in his brilliant eyes.

"I'm sure I meant it quite innocently." She blinked her thick lashes.

"I know you did." His beautiful mouth turned down. "You look like every man's dream, but you're still a little girl."

He was so close to her she could feel the heat of his body, his clean male fragrance filling her nostrils. It kept her unusually quiet. She couldn't adjust to this new Nick. Yet he was exactly the same, wasn't he? It was she who was changing.

"What are you thinking about?" he asked her as if he really wanted to know.

"Oh, I'm just plumbing the depths of my limited experience," she told him wryly. "Is it possible I don't really know you at all?"

"It's not so very long ago you were a child." He looked down at her lovely, shadowed face. "It isn't easy becoming a woman."

"No." She gave a shaken little sigh.

"Don't worry about it," his usually velvety voice went harsh. "You'll make it, I promise you."

Everything he said to her was coming from a distance because her ears were filled with the tumultuous pulsing of her blood. It was strange to be dancing with Nick, their hands touching. The most natural thing in the world in some way, yet spellbinding. She had known him since she was fourteen. Dynamic, mocking, caustic, charming Nick.

"You didn't ask Colin?" she accused him.

"I had enough of him the other night."

"He's nice," she said loyally, unable at that moment to recall Colin's face.

"Is that what you want from a man—*niceness*?" His hand speared into the thick weight of her hair so she had to lift her face to him.

"I don't know what I want," she said huskily, and shockingly tears leapt into her eyes. *Tears!* She could have died.

"Kendall!"

She heard the sharp intake of his breath and his arms tightened around her almost violently.

"It's all right. I'm not about to make a fool of myself." But she was.

"Steady—" He looked down at her in concern. "Your whole body is shaking."

Thalia Langford witnessed it too, her tall figure outlined against the light from the magnificent rock crystal chandelier that glittered in the room behind her.

"Nick!" she called with a frowning expression, "Senator and Mrs. Lawson have to leave now."

"God, I'd forgotten!" Nick muttered under his breath. "Stay here, Kendall. Don't go away."

Of course she did. The further away the better. What was happening to her? Was she going mad?

To calm herself she sought out her father, but he was in the middle of one of his funny stories and only pulled her down on to the side of his armchair. What was she supposed to say, anyway? I think I'm falling in love with Nick. How very messy that would be. Self-destructive. Nick would stop calling, Harry would lose a friend and Pamela a would-be backer. She had no option but to do her level best to avoid him for the rest of the night.

CHAPTER FOUR

THE next day Colin presented himself at the farm and invited her over to his place for lunch.

"Mother's asked a few people over," he explained with a gentle smile. "You can help me cook all the steaks."

"Your mother invited me, of course?"

"Insisted on it," said Colin. "Mother's very fond of you, you know that."

The last thing Kendall wanted to do was go over to the Hogans' for a barbecue, but at least it presented an escape route. Harry had somehow managed to speak to Nick about "a little business venture we're considering" and Nick had very obligingly promised he would call over and see them lateish the following afternoon. His guests would be gone by then.

She was certain of one thing: she didn't want to see Nick. Not now that she had recognised what she had always felt for him. For the very first time in her life she was afraid—afraid of herself and her hectically blossoming emotions.

It was three miles away to the Hogan farm and she arrived in time to see Sue Lockhart and her mother and father getting out of their car.

"Hi there!" Kendall called in her friendly fashion. The Lockharts were nice people, quiet and hard-working, who had settled very easily into the community. Kendall had no idea, though, they were particularly close to Mrs. Hogan.

"How nice to see you, dear!" smiled Mrs. Lockhart,

a pretty little woman in a sleeveless cotton frock.
"How's the family?"

"Fine." The girls exchanged smiles and hellos and
Mr. Lockhart caught them up, a tall lean man towering
over his wife and daughter. "Well, what do you know,
young Kendall! When are we going to see you over at
our place?"

"Just as soon as I can make it," she met his smiling
blue eyes. "You've no idea how we enjoy seeing your
plantation thrive."

"Yes, thank God!" Mr. Lockhart said earnestly. "In
another two years, we'll be able to harvest the mature
plants. I think I can promise you a good quality tea full
of flavour."

They all walked up to the house together, Kendall
continuing to ask Mr. Lockhart questions about his tea
plants that fascinated her, so she was hardly aware that
Sue was looking her over very thoroughly. Noting her
hair and her light make-up, the way the dark green of
her tube top, teamed with a gaily patterned skirt,
deepened the colour of her eyes. Sue was a pretty girl in
the same blue-eyed, fair-haired fashion as her mother
and she never had any particular wish to look vivid and
yes—*sexy*, until she saw Kendall.

There were four more people in the house, all friends
of Mrs. Hogan and long known to Kendall, so she stood
back while the introductions went on with the Lockharts. Mrs. Hogan kept her house spotless, but Kendall
always had the mad desire to ruffle up a few things.
There were no books lying around, no animals, just a
few flowers arranged stiffly in the wrong vases and all
the curtains pulled as though Mrs. Hogan feared what
all the brilliant sunshine would do to her many pieces of
rather heavy furniture and all the little knick-knacks
that stood about on tables and shelves. The *new* curtains, she noted, did nothing more for the room than
crowd it—such a dismal colour and pattern.

She must have been staring fixedly at the curtains, for Mrs. Hogan gave her a sharp-eyed glance. "What's the verdict, Kendall?"

"Very professional," she answered, neatly evading a more direct answer. Mrs. Hogan was very skilled with her needle, and she took the comment at face value because she looked pleased.

"Why don't you young people get the fire going," she said happily, "and I'll bring everything outside."

In the end, it was quite a pleasant day. Conversation never flagged in spite of the fact Mrs. Hogan didn't serve alcoholic beverages, and Colin behaved dutifully, dividing his time equally between Sue and Kendall. Sue, it was obvious, had what it took to be a favourite with Mrs. Hogan, and an outing was even suggested when Colin could take Sue to a beauty spot she had never visited.

"Why doesn't Kendall come too?" Sue said tactfully, and such generosity plucked at Kendall's heart strings, because it was quite clear Sue, with her gentle diffidence, had found a soulmate in Colin.

"I've seen it many times before." She smiled into the other girl's anxious blue eyes. "Go along and enjoy yourself—and take a swimsuit, because there's the most beautiful waterfall."

Seeing Kendall off at the car, Colin said thoughtfully, "What do you suppose Mother's trying to do? Sue's a nice girl, but she's nothing beside you."

"Why don't you give her a chance?" said Kendall. "I think you make her shy."

"Me, make a girl *shy*?" Colin threw back his head and laughed. "I suppose it won't be too bad, at that. She's a sweet little thing really, and Mother seems to like her."

"She does that," Kendall confirmed dryly. "Well, thank you for a lovely day, but I must get away."

"You never told me how you got on at Flamingo Park."

"You heard about it?" Kendall lifted her eyes to Colin's thin, tanned face, framed in the car window.

"Everyone hears about Nick's parties. How did it go?"

"An immense success," she said wryly.

"I guess it's a fabulous place?" Colin asked wistfully.

"It is, but never mind, you're doing pretty well yourself. The place looks great!"

"I'm coping better than I thought," Colin said with justifiable pride, "but then I have Mother."

Kendall didn't answer this, but just smiled. "Take care, and don't go breaking Sue's heart."

"I think she knows where my heart lies," Colin said more forcefully than usual. "I'll ring you later on in the week. We might go somewhere Wednesday night. That movie they made out of Miles Franklin's book got a good write-up."

"My Brilliant Career?" Kendall nodded swiftly. "I'd like that."

The storm that had been threatening for the past hour, and brought Mrs. Hogan's little gathering scurrying to their cars, suddenly broke. One minute the sun was shining brilliantly through the bank-up of clouds, the next, a tropical downpour. The windscreen wipers didn't work half fast enough and as she made her ascent up the crater road, Kendall considered pulling off altogether. The road got quite greasy in places and it was a series of bends.

She dropped speed looking for a likely place to pull off, and just as she did so, she saw a small, oncoming yellow car suddenly hurtle around the bend, moving outwards off the road as the driver lost control, then spin right around in a crazy skid.

It was right in front of her and, horrified, she knew she wouldn't be able to stop her own car in time. She had never had an accident in the year she had been driving, now it was happening right in front of her eyes.

The whole shocking nightmare took seconds, yet it might have been played out in slow motion. She hit her brakes, not too hard in case she put herself into a spin, and almost but not quite cleared the other vehicle. They collided with a terrific crunch and the yellow car nosed on a few more feet into a tree.

Kendall didn't feel anything then but relief. She was still in one piece even if her car wasn't, and the other driver was already getting out of his car. Her hands weren't even shaking as she pulled her own battered little vehicle off the road a short distance ahead. How unexpected life was: a party one moment, a prang the next.

She didn't even feel the rain, and neither apparently did the other driver. He was young, about her age, with a not particularly intelligent face.

"Strewth!" he gave a whistling breath. "That was close!"

"You're dead right!" she said flatly. "This is a dangerous road in the wet."

"I tried," he almost whined. "I tried to miss ya."

"You've got a cut on your head," she told him.

"Have I?" He put up his hand. "No matter. Me head's the least of me worries. "It's not *my car*."

"Who does it belong to?" She could feel water running down her back and the hollow between her breasts.

"Me mum." He suddenly started shouting. "She'll *kill* me!"

"You could have killed yourself *and* me," she said briskly. "Simmer down. I'll bet your mum would rather have you than the car."

"I feel...*sick*!"

"Oh dear!" He did look green. "Come back to your car. You'll be able to sit down."

"You're a cool one, aren't ya?" he said weakly a few minutes later, having been distressingly ill.

"It wouldn't do much good if I was anything else. Look, you'll have to wait here while I go and get help. You've damaged your radiator."

"Oh hell!" he muttered.

"Radiators are replaceable," she said comfortingly, thankful her own engine was to the rear. "I shouldn't be very long. I live about ten minutes away. My name's Kendall Reardon, by the way."

He shut his eyes. "Bobbie Cotton."

"Bobbie Cotton?" For some reason this struck her as very funny, and her voice held a mixture of pity and laughter. "Well, hang on in there, Bobbie, and I'll go for help."

When she arrived back at the farm, Nick was parked under the jacaranda at the side of the house. There were fallen blue-lavender blossoms all over the roof and hood of his car. It looked quite festive. Kendall tore up the steps, had the presence of mind to slip out of her soaked sandals, and called through the house.

"Harry, are you there?" She was soaked to the skin, but she didn't care much.

"What's up?" Harry came through to the verandah with Nick at his shoulder. "What the devil's been happening to you?" His astonished eyes ranged over her small, drenched-to-the-skin figure.

"There's been an accident."

"Not you?" Harry took a tottering step and fell into a chair. "You're all right, aren't you?"

Nick moved towards her. "You're not injured in any way, Kendall?" His black eyes were inspecting her inch by inch.

"No, it's the other feller!" She tried to joke, but now she seemed to be dissolving into jelly. "A few miles back. He's only young. He went into a skid and careened right around in front of me."

"I'll kill him," said Harry.

"I think his mum's going to do that."

"You'll have to get out of those wet things," said Nick as though what he said settled it.

"I told him I'd go back."

"Ridiculous!"

"Pam!" Harry yelled.

"If you're sure you're all right, Kendall," Nick said, still watching her like a hawk, "I'll go back and see what I can do for this young chap."

"He's busted his radiator."

"Come here, darling," Harry suddenly leapt up and enfolded her in a bear-hug. "My precious girl!"

"Now what?" Pamela came out on to the verandah to ask. They had been right in the midst of a very important discussion—for her.

"Kendall has had an accident," Nick explained rather shortly when usually he was very courteous. "I'd give her some sweetened tea and make her lie down. She's had a shock."

"My dear child!" Pamela hastened to her side, anxious to make up for her shortcomings. "Come with me."

Kendall wouldn't take to her bed, but she did allow Pamela to make her a cup of instant coffee with two heaped teaspoons of sugar. It was so sweet, she thought it would make her ill, when in fact just sipping it made her feel better. Later they all sat in the sun room that overlooked hill and valley and the Lockharts' tea plantation, and waited for Nick.

It was almost an hour before he was back and Pamela was looking at her watch. She and Harry had promised the "trendy" Jamiesons, friends of Nick's, that they would go over for dinner. Clive Jamieson had quite an art collection he particularly wanted Harry to see; not knowing that Harry had very little interest in artists other than himself and the greats.

"Silly young twit!" Nick sat down abruptly in a chair and looked at Kendall. "You must be feeling better, you have a little colour."

"I'm fine." She leaned her head back on the velvet cushion. "Thanks, Nick."

"God knows what we'd do without you," Harry said with real feeling. "I hope you gave him a good talking to."

"I opted out when his mother arrived," Nick said crisply, then gave a sardonic laugh in remembrance.

"Did you have to call the police?" asked Pamela, pretending interest.

"Not enough damage. They were both lucky."

"Lucky!" Kendall groaned. "Have you seen my car?"

"More or less," Nick returned a little tartly.

"Well, you know what they say, all's well that ends well," Harry said more cheerfully. "I daresay we can bash the dints out."

"Leave it to me," Nick glanced at Kendall briefly. "I'll get someone to pick it up at the mill. I can easily find you another little runabout in the meantime."

"Are you always so generous to your friends?" she found herself asking almost challengingly.

"No." His black gaze flashed to her face, a rather unnerving glance.

"Well, on behalf of all of us, Nick," Harry bounded into the fray, "I'd like to say we very much appreciate it. Kendall would be lost without her little car. By the way, you'd better ring the Jamiesons," Harry suddenly added to his wife.

"Whatever for?" Her meticulously darkened eyebrows shot up.

"I don't like to leave Kendall after she's had an accident!" Harry exclaimed.

"But she's perfectly all right." Pamela began to bristle even in front of Nick. "Besides, it's much too late to ring them now. We're expected in just over an hour.''

"Don't put it off." Nick looked at Kendall with an expressionless face. "I'll be happy to look after your little wee lamb."

"I can look after myself!" Kendall protested before her emotions got the better of her.

"It doesn't look like it," Nick said unfairly. "I'm having a quiet night. You can come back with me. You told me yourself you haven't seen over the whole house."

"There now, that's settled!" Harry's rugged face crinkled into a delightful smile. "There's only one man I'd trust with my daughter, Nick, and that's you."

Pamela drew a breath of deepest regret; she hadn't seen over the entire house either. "If you're sure, Nick."

"Hey, listen here," Kendall cried, all prickles, "I don't need a baby-sitter!"

"You're getting one regardless!" said Nick with lazy arrogance. "I don't expect you to thank me."

The storm had passed into the ranges by the time they reached Flamingo Park, and Kendall took a deep, sweet breath of air.

"Fancy having the honour to be asked back a second time!"

"Don't keep needling me, little one," he warned her, amused and a little angry. "I know I tricked you into this, but you have nothing to worry about."

"Such as?" The entrance hall was even more beautiful when the house was quiet and empty of swarming people.

"Whatever was bothering you last night!" The corners of his mouth quirked.

She didn't dare face him, but walked ahead into the drawing room while Nick flicked on the lights. "Just

because I was enjoying myself with Dave Masterson!''
Any excuse was better than none.

"Did you absolutely need to run away?"

Whatever she did she had to conceal from him her
personal tragedy. Because that, in fact, was what it
could become. "This is some inheritance," she said,
"you're going to bequeath to your son."

"It really needs a house full of children," he remarked, and glanced at her expressionless profile.

"But remember what Harry says, you have to get
married first."

"I've even found the woman."

"I'm sure you didn't have to look far." The pain of it
nearly doubled her over.

"That's about the size of it!" Surprisingly, his voice
sounded amused. "Stop drifting about aimlessly, Kendall, and let me show you all those other rooms you
wanted to know about."

She went quietly, visiting rooms one by one, such big
rooms, with high ceilings, all handsomely and appropriately furnished. She had never seen so many
beautiful plastered ceilings festooned with fruits and
flowers and scrolls, so much stained glass and elegant
chandeliers. The furniture was almost uniformly antique throughout the house, except for the custom-made
settees and deep, comfortable armchairs, and there were
dozens of rich-looking Persian rugs decorating the
floors.

The woman who became mistress of this would be
very fortunate indeed, though all her life Thalia Langford had been used to riches. So that was it—Thalia
Langford. Apparently they weren't worried about being
cousins.

"Where's Mrs. Mitchell?" she asked idly. Nora
Mitchell had been in the Langford service for years, a
completely efficient woman who now ran the house for
him.

"Really, Kendall," he said lightly, "she's entitled to some time off—especially after last night."

"You mean we're on our own?" She turned away from the absorbed contemplation of a distinguished marble bust of the Hon. John Palmer Langford. He had Nick's arrogant nose and cleft chin.

"So what?" he arched one black brow. "I'm not a notorious rapist."

"And you're almost engaged to be married—right?"

"It might take longer than I think. Come downstairs, you silly child. I think you need feeding."

They were half way through an excellent impromptu meal that Nick had insisted on preparing for them when the phone rang.

"Excuse me," Nick said unhurriedly, and walked away to take it in his study.

When he came back he looked at her levelly. "That was Thalia."

"Keeping check on you already?" Kendall fairly gulped her Beaujolais.

"I'm afraid so," Nick settled back into his chair again, looking not the least perturbed. "Eat up."

There was no doubt about it, now. He had practically admitted it.

The food turned to ashes; the red wine to gall. They had been discussing Pamela's idea for her shop (Kendall didn't bother to say it had been *her* idea, and neither apparently had Harry), so she clung to that topic as if it were her salvation.

"It's important to you, isn't it?" Nick asked abruptly, looking at the serious intentness of her face.

"I think it would be good for all of us, most importantly Pamela."

"Very well," Nick shrugged.

Her green eyes grew huge. "I'm not asking *you* to help, Nick. Just your advice."

"Don't get so agitated," he said, and helped her away

from the table. "It just so happens I share your belief that Pamela could make a go of it, and the market is there."

"But Nick, *please*," in her embarrassment she grabbed hold of his arm, "I'm sure a bank or a finance company would back Pamela."

"Darling," he spoke a little harshly, "neither Harry nor Pamela have any capital to support their proposition." He didn't seem aware he had used any form of endearment, though it had only been used in hard mockery.

"Oh, damn you, Nick!" She felt like crying they had come to depend on him so much.

"Shut up!"

She couldn't take it calmly. "Does Harry know you're going to back Pamela yourself?"

"No, he doesn't know yet."

"What if anything goes wrong?" she protested, her green eyes sparkling like emeralds.

"Then I'll take *you* for security," Nick put out his hand and curled a thick strand of her hair around his finger.

"You're cruel!" It was inexpressibly frightening to see sensuality flare into his eyes.

"Why, what have I done to you?"

She wouldn't, couldn't, set the match to her own immolation. "You make me feel as though we're imposing on you frightfully," she told him more quietly. "It was just an idea Pamela had."

"I've a feeling it was *yours*." He took her hand and led her out on to the terrace. "Don't worry about it, Kendall. I'll see that it's all set up properly. It's not as risky as you seem to think, otherwise I'd have to say no. Pamela has great personal flair in her dressing and other women are aware of it. For instance, she looked a knock-out last night. If *she* tells them what looks good on them and has the top quality stock the women of the district would be happy enough to pay up in their own town. The money is around, but none of the shops in town are anyway near classy enough for, say, Thalia and her circle.''

''And they're paying hundreds of dollars more just to fly out and get what they want,'' Kendall added, gazing out over the idyllic setting; the lush walls of flowering hedges and vines, the sloping lawn and the ingenious way the huge swimming pool had been constructed to resemble a natural lake. It must have cost a fortune, but it had tremendous aesthetic appeal. There was a tennis court too to the rear of the garden, completely shielded from the house by a towering wall of white bougainvillea. Nick had occasionally given her a game there, but as he unkindly told her, he could beat her with one hand tied behind his back. He could too, and she had to endure it.

''It's all so fantastically peaceful,'' she said fervently. ''A private world.''

''It's only a small corner of it,'' Nick told her dryly.

''When does the annual sale come up? It must be soon.''

''The twenty-sixth of the next month,'' Nick confirmed. ''I'll be offering some of the best bulls in the country and a couple of hundred heifers.''

''And how's Frank?'' Frank Delance was Nick's longstanding manager.

''He's out of plaster, but he'll never be able to live down getting thrown from a horse. Which reminds me, you haven't been riding for some time.''

''The weekend just flies,'' she shook her head.

''Particularly when you spend most of it peddling fruit at the front door.'' A shadow of anger passed across his autocratic dark face.

''Damn it, am I supposed to be ashamed of it?'' she demanded resentfully.

"I've already spoken to Harry," he told her. "There'll be no more!"

"You bully!" She was ruffled out of all proportion by his assumption of power.

"I guess I am," he said, looking down at her. "Now you know it, we'll get along just fine."

Kendall turned away abruptly and moved down towards the pool, trying unsuccessfully to conquer the excitement and anger that was digging into her like great talons. She knew how impossible it was to go against Nick, now more than ever when he had determined on being Pamela's silent partner. Frowning, she looked into the water, hearing Nick's cool, crisp voice saying beside her,

"What are you getting yourself so upset for? You're getting harder to handle than a filly with a bloodline a mile long!"

"All right, so I am. Do stop *going on* about it!" She made herself turn to face him and as she did her high-heeled sandal slipped on the pool surround and with a frantic little cry she overbalanced and went in the deep end.

When she surfaced, Nick was laughing and already holding out his hand. "I guess it took something to cool you down."

"Maybe I wanted to," she called in a taut voice.

"Come on out!"

"Now I'm here I might as well pound up a few lengths." She turned about and struck out for the steps at the other end. She was quite obviously a stylish swimmer, but by the time she got to the beautiful river boulders, she was breathless.

Quickly Nick hauled her out, supporting her while she momentarily sagged against him. "That was *your* fault!" she said raggedly.

"This just isn't your day. Surely you remember it's been raining." Paying no attention at all to his own expensive clothes, he lifted her up in his arms and walked with her back into the house.

"Put me down," Kendall protested. "It doesn't matter where."

"God, you're so young you make my heart ache!" He glanced down at her golden-skinned face. "This is the second time today I've seen you drenched."

"And obviously it amused you. Just give me a towel."

"I'll do better than that."

Despite her protests he carried her with athletic grace to the most beautiful of the upstairs bedrooms that had its own adjoining bathroom. "I think you'll find all you need here." He put her on her feet and smiled. "This is my mother's room. She always uses it when she comes to visit me."

"Oh!" Hastily Kendall moved to the tiled floor of the bathroom. "She's very beautiful, isn't she, your mother." Kendall had only seen Nick's mother once, but she had never forgotten. She lived in Melbourne now with her second husband, a well-known financier.

"I think so." Nick slid open the mirrored door of a series of built-in wardrobes that ran the full width of the room. "You should be able to find something to put on. Liz is a lot taller than you are, but she's very slim."

"Go away, Nick," she begged him. "As soon as I've got something dry on, I'm going home."

"Why?" he asked briefly, his black eyes sardonic.

"Because. . . ." she floundered, "because it's the intelligent thing to do."

"You surprise me sometimes," said Nick with mock gravity, but he did leave her in peace.

Agitation lent wings to her movements. She stripped off her wet things, rolled them in a towel and draped another one around her. She couldn't blame Nick if he thought her a perfect fool. Her hair would take ages to dry, it was so thick and heavy, but when she opened a drawer she found a very efficient hair dryer.

She gave her hair a quick all-over blast of hot air, seeing it mass into deep waves and curls, but she thought she oughtn't waste any more time on it. If Nick took her home in a few minutes she would be safely there before Harry and Pamela arrived back.

When she moved back into the bedroom she saw that most of the clothes in the wardrobe, though beautiful, were not suitable for going home in, let alone for Nick's eyes. It was mostly bedroom wear, satins and chiffons and the most beautiful green silk dressing gown with a shawl collar and brilliantly embroidered on the shoulders and patch pockets. If she belted it tightly, it just might do. It would *have* to do, failing a trench coat.

The kimono would have been three-quarter length on a tall woman, but on Kendall it came down to her toes. She couldn't put her sandals on again, so she tucked them into the towel as well.

"Kendall?" Nick tapped on the door. "Come on!" He sounded as though he meant it too.

She rushed for the door and threw it open. "Finally I'm ready." It was her habit to be flippant and mildly bantering with Nick, but some expression on his down-bent face prevented her from adding, "How do I look?"

"I guess you know green is your colour."

Run, Kendall whispered to herself. *Pick up your feet and run!*

"What about driving me home?" she said instead.

"You look very much at home already." There was a bitter-sweet half smile on his handsome mouth and she said a little shakily:

"You just remember, Nick, I'm eighteen years old."

"I know. It's a bit of a problem. Come on then, before your eyes swallow up your face."

She made it quite safely downstairs, but when he

turned unexpectedly to address a remark to her she
visibly flinched away. It was a mistake—a big one, for
his black eyes flashed anger.

"What the hell is going on?" he demanded.

The colour flew into her face, staining her cheekbones. "Nothing, Nick!" she quavered.

"Maybe you think I'm looking for a few kicks?"

His tone was so cutting and contemptuous she found
herself growing angry. "You might if you got bored
enough."

"You impertinent little bitch!" He hauled her right
up against him and her towelled bundle dropped right
out of her nerveless hand.

"Don't you dare, Nick!" His grip hurt her and she
began to struggle.

"But I thought we were such friends."

"The hell we are!" She was struggling impotently.
"It's not liking I feel for you."

"What is it then—fear?" He held her implacably.
"For God's sake, you don't really want me to hurt you,
do you?"

"And when have you ever passed up the chance?"
She was going right over the edge, but she couldn't stop.
This was *it*; her hidden terror that she would goad Nick
into arousal.

His fingers biting into her skin through the thin,
heated satin sent shock waves jolting right through her
trembling body, so her colour failed and her green eyes
glittered like jewels.

"What a little coward you are," he said harshly.
"You can't act the hysterical little virgin for ever. One
has to get to know about life instead of running away
from it."

"That's what they all say," she hurled at him, "the
expert seducers. I'm telling you, Nick Langford, touch
me and I'll scream!"

"Of course you *could*, but you won't." He pinned

her glistening head with his hand. "The truth is, you lit-tle witch, you've been trying to bring me around to kiss-ing you for some time."

"You crazy man!" Sheer rage overcame her terror and she threw back her head so the sudden, wincing pain brought tears to her eyes. "Oh, you—you damned men! Listen here, you conceited oaf...."

His mouth covered hers so savagely he almost cut off her breath for ever. For a few frightening seconds she thought she would faint dead away, and maybe she did faint, for when she came to her senses she was lying in his arms on the high-backed chesterfield sofa and the cruel pressure of his mouth had given way to a deep, penetrating exploration.

It wasn't even surrender, but a merciless subjugation.

She wanted to cry *rape* and what's the penalty, but there was no way she could free herself of this ravishing violation.

Dazedly she wondered how, hating him, she could love him at the same time. Her heart was beating tu-multuously against her ribs and she didn't know that the shawled collar of the jade robe had come apart and the light gleamed on her small, golden breasts, the rosy tips standing erect in arousal.

A stirring was in her now that couldn't be denied. She shuddered in a kind of anguished acceptance and Nick held her more closely while the stirring moved relentless-ly all over her body, wave after wave of it, storming her defenses and dragging her under.

She couldn't even think of the light and meaningless caresses she had received in the past. This was destruc-tion, and it had been waiting for her for a long time.

She must have been muttering incoherent little in-cantations, for he lifted his head in an attempt to hear her. "Kendall?" His voice, normally so dark and decisive, was very faintly slurred.

She couldn't answer him or even open her eyes. She

was reeling in mind and body with only the strength to twist her head away, but Nick put his hand under the side of her face and forced her head back to him.

"I can hear your heart beating. You haven't died."

The last vestige of pride remained to her. She realised then what he was offering her: physical ecstasy, but nothing of himself. It was like a stab wound to the heart. Her eyes flew open, but she was so dizzy she could hardly see.

"I hate you!" she whispered passionately.

"Well, it's surely not love. Maybe a virus. You'll get over it." He looked down at her face, her lovely mouth, the gleaming young breasts, and his hand moved as though he no longer had full control over it, cupping her breast, while the tips of his fingers teased the dusky nipple.

"Nick, *please*!" she murmured frantically, even as her body arched towards him instinctively.

"What are you feeling? Tell me." His voice had gone husky.

"*Shame*. I hate it—I *do*!" She had to close her eyes again, because she couldn't let him see she was frantic with yearning. It was impossible. All of it—the desperate urgency, the pain.

He didn't let her go, but kept her pinned down, his tender-hard mouth brushing exploratively all over her skin. Backwards and forwards, his hand on her breast.

She had the feeling the whole thing was a dark dream that had caught them both up, a fantasy, impossibly erotic. God knows how it would all have ended, but the phone rang again, stridently, over and over.

Alienated, she wrenched away and there were tears on her cheeks. "It's Thalia," she said wildly, "she's discovered if she gets a pair of binoculars...."

Nick lifted her up like a bundle of feathers and threw her back on the sofa. "Personally I believe it's the Almighty."

When he came back again, Kendall was standing in the middle of the entrance hall, trembling violently. "Well?"

"My uncle," he murmured, and gave her a piercing look. "Feel all right?"

"From now on I'm getting busy with my prayers," she said sharply. "I can just imagine what a fate worse than death would be like at your hands."

"I'm sorry!" Almost tenderly he reached out and stroked back a thick swathe of her hair. "Even a gentleman such as I can become bewitched."

"Take me home, Nick." She suddenly felt like weeping hysterically. "And never, never, *never* kiss me again!"

CHAPTER FIVE

FOR the next few days she did her work like an automaton, trying desperately to keep her mind a blank. Up until now, except for the terrible blow of losing her mother, her life had been fairly uncomplicated. She worried about Harry, of course, and she had no meaningful relationship with Pamela or ever could, but the past few years had been relatively calm. Now *this*! Despite her most determined efforts her mind kept going back to the thrilling time she had spent in Nick's arms—not thrilling as in radiant happiness, but a fearful, throbbing ravishment. She was madly, no, *insanely*, in love with him, and the pain and humiliation it could bring her put her on her mettle.

On the Wednesday evening, selfishly, she almost invited Colin's gentle, tentative caresses, but that too was a mistake, because it provoked an unaccustomed burst of ardour.

"You understand how I feel about you, don't you, Kendall?" Colin asked with his cheek on her hair.

"You're a little in love with me," she said gently, ashamed of herself now.

"I want to marry you!" He grabbed her face between his hands. "Oh, please, Kendell, if you say yes, I'll wait for you for ever!"

"But, Colin," she said despairingly. "I've told you the thought of marriage leaves me cold. Don't you see all the divorces in the newspaper?"

"Well, we can't live together," he said, considerably

taken aback. "I know you're frightened of commitment, but then you've had a very unsettled life."

"Damn it, I haven't!" She jerked away angrily.

"Mother says you have."

He said it in such a prim, matter-of-fact voice, Kendall could have screamed. "What your mother knows about me or my life would fill a pin's head!"

"Oh, Kendall!" Colin exclaimed, shocked and at the same time, sympathetic. "She really likes you, you know and she's most concerned about your welfare."

"God knows *I've* missed it," Kendall retorted with a little wry grimace. "The fact is, Colin, and I think you're making yourself purposely blind to the situation, your mother dislikes me intensely and always has."

"It's late," said Colin, "you must be tired."

"As it happens I am. I haven't been sleeping well, but you'd better believe what I say. Your mother would welcome almost anyone as a daughter-in-law before me."

"You're crazy!" Colin protested. "My mother lives for me. She only wants to see me happy."

"But not with me," Kendall said tiredly. "In any case, dear friend, though I'm very fond of you, I'm hanging out for Prince Charles."

"I'll do," said Colin. "You'll see."

At the weekend she accepted an invitation of Dave Masterson's to go dancing and the next day went with him to the beach. Dave was good company, happy and uncomplicated, and they spent a very enjoyable day together. Or at least it filled her waking hours. He was nothing like Nick, nobody could be that, but he had a quick humour and a self-assurance she liked. Also, and more pertinently in his favour, he had no intention of settling down until he was in his late twenties. Or so he told her.

When they got back from the beach, Nick's car was parked in its usual spot at the side of the house and

Kendall turned to Dave with a brilliant, beguiling smile.

"You're coming in, aren't you?"

"Love it!" Dave was already out the door. "That father of yours tells the funniest stories."

Harry greeted them in his usual cheerful manner. Pamela smiled very cordially and Nick rose lazily, his black eyes moving indulgently over both of them.

"How was the surf?"

"Terrific!" Dave's hazel eyes shone. "This girl can even ride a board."

"You'll stay for a bite of tea, won't you, son?" Harry asked affably. "Nothing fancy, grilled chops or something."

"I think we can do better than *that*, darling," Pamela corrected him.

"Chuck a possum on the fire," said Harry, not to be outdone.

As it happened, Kendall with a little stage-managing from an unusually benign Pamela put on a perfectly acceptable meal; an avocado appetiser, peppered steaks served with zucchini and tomatoes and some tiny new potatoes tossed in butter and fresh herbs, and because there wasn't time to do much about a dessert, she peeled some bananas, put them in a buttered baking dish, poured a heated brown sugar, orange juice, spices and sherry mixture over the lot and popped it in the oven. It only took about ten minutes and Harry liked heated rum poured on afterwards and the dish set alight.

Pamela very obligingly whipped the cream. "Nick's being absolutely marvellous!" she confided. "God knows how we're ever going to repay him."

"By being a big success."

"Honestly, I've got that many ideas!"

"Steady!" Kendall put her hand on Pamela's whirring arm. She was turning the cream to butter.

"It's so terribly exciting!" Pamela's blue eyes glittered in the kitchen light. "If we can get the Langford women interested, we're *made*!"

"They're not the only ones with money," Kendall pointed out, flushed from the oven.

"They're the ones that matter," Pamela told her a little sharply. "By the way, did you know it's almost official Nick and his cousin Thalia are getting engaged?"

"How disgusting!" Kendall said abruptly, turning away. "Who told you anyway?" She wouldn't believe it. *Wouldn't*, until she knew it was true.

"Why, Thalia's mother!" Pamela looked at her with real surprise. Kendall rarely spoke so gruffly. "I was speaking to her at the party and she dropped the hint."

"Wishful thinking, I'd say," Kendall filled the percolator. "Mothers being what they are."

"You're so right!" Pamela breathed deeply, transported momentarily back to her girlhood. "Anyway, I don't think she's half good enough for him. She's not even good-looking, unless you like horses. Still, I suppose she dresses well. She does have a certain style."

Kendall pretended to take it all very calmly, but inside she was a jangling mass of nerves. Probably the easiest course was to stay outside in the kitchen, but she couldn't hide all her life.

"Gosh, you're a beautiful cook!" Dave exclaimed over coffee. "That was one of the best meals I've ever tasted!"

"Nothing my little girl can't do," said Harry, smiling tenderly at his daughter. "Of course I can show her a thing or two, I'm a pretty good cook myself."

"He is too!" Pamela was giving a splendid portrayal of a happy, devoted wife. "We just might be able to open a little restaurant next to the shop."

When Dave left, Kendall walked down with him to the car. It was a beautiful night, warm and balmy with the moon riding high over the farm. She usually loved such a night, only now the night reminded her of Nick, the scented dark and being alone with him in the car. She still had his mother's kimono hidden at the back of her closet. She couldn't bear to look at it, or give it back either.

"Thanks a lot, Kendall," Dave took her hand. "I've really enjoyed myself."

"I'm glad."

"Not just tonight," he pressed his thumb into her palm, "the whole weekend. I had this idea you were going steady with Colin Hogan?"

"I'm not going steady with anyone," she pointed out firmly.

"Atta girl!" He laughed, bent his red head and kissed her cheek. "What about coming over next weekend to my place? Mamma thought you were absolutely lovely at Nick's party. Dad, too, of course, but we can take that for granted."

"I'd like that." She smiled at him. Colin couldn't question her loyalty. He was taking Sue Lockhart to Silverspring.

"Great!" Dave, forgetting his rule not to get too deeply involved with girls, suddenly tipped up her face and kissed her thoroughly on the mouth. "You're some girl, you know that?"

On a wave of well-being he jumped into his Porsche and sped away with an exuberant honk of his horn at the gate.

Nick was on the verandah, looking out over the tangled jungle of the garden. "Pretty hard on poor old Dave, isn't it?" he drawled.

"God, you're a sarcastic beast!"

"Can't do much about it now." He caught her arm as she went to flounce past him. "Keep me company. Harry and Pamela are doing the washing up."

"Good grief!" If Pamela wasn't careful she would sprout a halo.

"Don't bother them. They seem to be closer together than usual."

"Thanks to you." Kendall had to say it because it was true. "Pamela is thrilled about what you're doing for her."

"Sorry—for *you*."

"For *me*?" She said it weakly, because Nick had taken her hand and led her to a chair.

"Me too. I expect this venture to pay off." He didn't sit down but leaned against the white timber railing studying her. She was pale under her tan and her green eyes were immense. "What's Colin going to say when he hears you've been gallivanting with young Dave?"

"I won't tell him."

"He'll hear about it!" He sounded coolly amused. The light from the hallway was on his hands—beautiful hands, clever and strong, hands that could bring a woman ecstasy. Kendall shivered uncontrollably. "Surely you're not cold?" Nick stepped a little nearer her, his shadow falling across her body.

"No." She drew back tautly. "Dave asked me over to his place next weekend."

"Go. You'll enjoy yourself," he nodded agreeably. "But spare poor old Colin the details."

"Colin has asked me to marry him," she said, and extended a hand in welcome to Sebastian who had run up the front steps.

"When?" Nick asked softly, and clicked his fingers at the German shepherd, who went to him instantly.

"Traitor!" Kendall breathed a sigh and lay back in her chair. "He told me he's prepared to wait."

"Not by the river, I hope," said Nick, and gave a brief laugh. "Why don't you put the poor devil out of his misery? You'd be hopelessly mismatched and while you keep him hoping he can't get on with the business of finding the girl who *could* make him happy."

She sat forward abruptly and stared at him. "You sound just like his dear mother!"

"You can't blame Mrs. Hogan for wanting the best for her son. You'll be a mother yourself one day."

"I don't know about that!" She laughed almost bitterly.

"Oh yes, you will!" Nick glanced at her, cruel and triumphant. "How else can you show a man you love him other than giving him his heart's desire—a son?"

Pain laced itself strongly about her heart. "How old are you, Nick?" she asked.

"Thirty-two to your eighteen." Impatient, a little amused.

"Then don't try and marry me off. You're not mad to lose your freedom yourself."

"I'm coming round to it," he said lightly. "Maybe a marriage of convenience and hope the love grows afterwards."

She couldn't stand any more, the hints, so she jumped to her feet, her skirt hampering her as it caught on a splinter of wood just under the seat.

"Damn, damn, *damn*!" She felt helpless and agitated.

"Hold still, you silly infant!" Very gently he set her free, and as she looked down he looked up into her face. "Don't weep."

She blinked the furious tears away. "I won't." Her head was spinning with his nearness, and he recognised it, knowing everything about women. He found the nape of her neck with his hand, apparently intent on making her betray herself, but Harry came through to the hallway singing the Toreador Song from *Carmen*, in a lusty, surprisingly good baritone.

"Ah, there you are!" he broke off to exclaim. "All finished. The little woman is just putting the dishes away."

"Then I'll go and say goodnight," Nick said

pleasantly. "I have an early start in the morning. I'm flying to Colby Downs."

They all walked out to the car to see him off and Pamela kissed his cheek affectionately. "We can't thank you enough, Nick. You've opened a whole new life for me."

"I'll be in touch." He hunted up his car keys and slid behind the wheel. "If you're not doing anything, Harry, you could come with me tomorrow if you like. We'd be back early evening."

"Say, that's a great idea!" Harry's eyes flashed enthusiasm. "I'm currently very interested in painting horses."

"Then make it over by about six. I'll be taking the Beech Baron."

"Give it a thorough check beforehand," Harry joked.

"See you later, pal!" Nick held up his hand. "Bye, Pamela...Kendall."

"That's a miracle of a car, isn't it?" Harry said happily as they walked back up the steps. "I always think the Jaguar is kind of unique."

"Then I'll buy you one!" Pamela put her arm about his waist. "I'll work my fingers to the bone."

"Naturally," Harry laughed. "I think Nick will expect it."

AROUND SEVEN the next evening, while they were delaying the evening meal until Harry returned, the phone rang.

"I'll get it," said Pamela. "It's probably Harry." She had been in a very good mood all day, so when she returned to the sun porch Kendall was shocked to see her classic face drained of all colour and life.

"What is it?" She stood up so quickly she knocked her sewing box off the table.

"It's Harry."

"Daddy!" Kendall's hand went to her throat.

"He had some kind of sick turn in Colby and Nick's calling the doctor to him now."

"Where are they?" Kendall's heart began to race with fear and panic.

"At home, at Nick's place." Pamela looked ghastly, and if there had been any doubt she loved Harry, there was none now. "We'll have to go to him."

"I'll get the car out." Kendall flew to the door.

The doctor was still with Harry when they arrived, but Pamela ran on upstairs.

"Oh, Nick!" Kendall had driven over, but now she felt she couldn't stand on her own feet.

"It's all right," Nick pulled her into his arms and kept them around her. "There's treatment for everything. I even spoke to him earlier about having a check-up."

"It's not his heart?" She looked up straight into his eyes.

"I don't know, Kendall," he answered seriously. "Dr. Richardson will tell us about that."

"If anything happened to Harry I couldn't bear it," she whispered, and her eyes filled with frightened tears.

"Don't *look* like that!" Nick seemed infected by her anguish. "Harry's of an age when a man has to take a little more care of himself. I'm sure that's all it is. He simply overdid it today. You know what he's like—he fairly gallops along."

"Kendall! Nick!" Pamela called to them from the gallery over the stairway. "Come up!" There was colour in her face, and it gave Kendall the strength to get up the stairs.

Harry was lying in an antique fourposter, his ruddy complexion robbed of tone, but a big smile on his face. "Come and kiss your dear father!" He held out his arms to Kendall. "If I hadn't tried riding a bronco today I'd have been perfectly all right."

Kendall flew across the room like an anguished child, and it was left to Nick and Pamela to talk to the distinguished-looking grey-haired man who stood near the window, shutting his bag.

It wasn't Harry's heart; the heart was beating strongly, but it wouldn't be for long if he wasn't treated immediately for his high blood pressure.

"I'm telling you, man," Dr. Richardson had said to him, "if you don't do something about this, and do it now, you're a candidate for a heart attack or a stroke!"

"Why, he had the cheek to tell me I had to lose thirty pounds!" Harry told them as soon as Dr. Richardson had gone.

"I hope you're going to do it, Daddy!" Kendall said earnestly.

"Oh, he'll do it all right," Pamela confirmed, the light of battle in her eyes. "If I can watch my figure so can Harry. And that takes care of the whisky!"

"So be it," said Harry, compliant for now. In actual fact he had given himself a tremendous fright, but the test would come when the fright had abated.

"There's a prescription to be filled." Nick turned away to the bedside table and picked up a script.

"I'll get it!" Kendall offered immediately.

"You can come with me," Nick told her. "I don't want you driving into town on your own." He rubbed his chin, his eyes on Pamela's concerned profile. "I think Harry had better stay where he is for the rest of the night."

"No, old chum. I've caused you enough trouble as it is." Harry sat up with a complexion like mud.

"Nick's right!" Pamela caught his fumbling hand. "Lie still and behave yourself."

"You're all very welcome to stay." Nick folded the script, put it in his breast pocket and moved to the door. "You'll only worry if you go home anyway."

"That's very kind of you, Nick!" Pamela said appreciatively.

"I'll go back home," said Kendall firmly. "Daddy has you both, and Sebastian will be lonely."

"Dear Jehovah!" Nick groaned. "Sebastian will survive for the night!"

"So what do I wear to work?" She glanced down at her casual sundress.

"Don't go." Nick fixed her with a stare. "It will take us thirty minutes to get into town, so let's go."

In the car they really moved along and she relaxed her spine. "Do you think he's going to do it?" she asked like a child begging for reassurance.

"What the doctor's ordered, you mean?"

"Yes. Harry's a big man. He likes to eat and drink. He'll find it very difficult to keep to a stringent diet."

"It's the drinking that really bothers me." Nick kept his eyes on the road ahead.

"He didn't always drink so heavily," Kendall said protestingly. "It's just become a habit since my mother died."

"He really misses her, doesn't he?" said Nick.

"He told you?" She turned her head in surprise. Though Harry loved to talk he very rarely mentioned anything that cut close to him.

"Strangely enough he spoke to me about your mother today. He loved her very deeply."

"She should never have died." Kendall turned her head away. "Why do people have to die when they're young?"

"Who can answer that?" Nick's dark profile was serious. "Harry appears to be succumbing to a kind of melancholia. He told me he thought his life was falling into ruin."

"Oh, *no!*" Kendall gave a distressed little gasp. "He couldn't have said that."

"He did. Under the comedian is a very sad man."

"I know that. I know my own father!" Kendall dashed the sudden tears from her eyes. "But he can't just pack it all in. He's only fifty years old."

"Maybe that's part of it." Nick answered quietly. "His age. Many men and women suffer from depression when they feel their best years are over. His drinking provides him with a false euphoria. He'll find it difficult to quit unless he gets himself in hand. The decision is his, to get some meaning and purpose into his life or shorten it through deliberate neglect."

"But didn't you talk to him?" Kendall asked worriedly.

"I did, very determinedly as it happens, but whether he'll listen is another thing again."

"He'll listen." Kendall clasped her hands together tightly in her lap. "You have a talent for making people listen."

"Sometimes you find that a mortal sin," Nick offered gravely. "You know Harry relies on you too much?"

"Surely he can love his only child?" She moved restively.

"Lots of parents love their children, but they don't keep them chained to their side. Harry is using you as a crutch and it's not right for you or him. In a way, it's even a serious threat to his marriage."

"Oh, hush!" Kendall put her hands over her ears. "The terrible things you say to me, Nick!"

"You *know* he should be turning to Pamela more. She's not a fool and there must be many times she feels shut out."

"So what do you want me to do?" she asked bitterly, "leave my own home?"

"It wouldn't have been a bad idea for you to have gone off to university. Don't forget I read all your report cards."

"I didn't *want* to go," she said fiercely.

"And Harry was determined to keep you home at all costs. Love can be very selfish."

"It was no sacrifice at all." She bent her cloudy dark head. "Pamela really loves him, you know. I was never really sure until tonight."

"I'd say it took a fright for her to show it. Pamela doesn't give much away either. It must be hell to be in competition with a ghost."

"I suppose so!" Kendall's laugh was as brittle as glass. "My mother didn't want Harry to grieve for her for ever. She loved him so much she always put his happiness first."

"And she was a big power in his life. Without her he seems to have lost all motivation in his work. He could be a fine painter, of the first rank, but it's obvious to all of us, including himself, that he's lost dedication. He doesn't even believe in himself any more."

They drove in silence after that, each thinking their own thoughts. In the town Nick parked opposite the all-night pharmacy, then turned to her briefly. "Sit there. It shouldn't take long."

Long enough, she thought, seeing at least a half a dozen people standing about waiting for prescriptions to be filled. People always seemed to get sick at night.

Five minutes went by and she pressed the interior light button on to check on the time. Almost eight o'clock. Nick had cassettes in the car, but she wanted to be quiet with her jangled nerves. Of course Harry depended on her too much, but what was she supposed to do? She scarcely earned enough to set herself up in anything very much outside a slum, and she didn't fancy that. The other alternative, and it seemed just as bad, was to marry Colin and be stuck with Mrs. Hogan for the rest of her life.

She began to torment herself with impossible courses of action, so deep in her misery she nearly jumped out of her skin when a tall female figure swooped like a vulture to the open car window and settled there.

"I *thought* it was you!" The tone couldn't have been more hostile or accusing.

"Oh, hello!" Kendall looked up startled into Thalia Langford's face.

"And what are *you* doing here?" The inquisition went on.

"Waiting for Nick."

"You mean you're out with him?" Thalia shrieked incredulously. There were sequins on her black jersey shift and they looked like a thousand accusing eyes.

"Not at all!" Kendall corrected her smartly. "He ran me in to the chemist. I didn't realise he had to ask your permission."

"Funny!" Thalia gave an unpleasantly tight little laugh. "You people really are the limit, aren't you, the way you impose on him. I've heard all about the little business venture."

"Have you?" Kendall wasn't surprised. "Then you'll surely agree it's going to be a success. Nick knows what he's doing."

"So apparently does your stepmother!" Thalia threw back her head like an unruly horse. "I didn't think anyone could con Nick."

"Nobody has," Kendall answered as evenly as she could. "My stepmother has what it takes to make a success of this thing. She has a brilliant flair for fashion and she was once a top model."

"What, twenty years ago?" Thalia sneered.

"Closer to ten." Kendall's hand clenched into a small fist, but it was scarcely ladylike to poke Thalia right on her interfering nose. "And that included London, Paris and Rome. No one in this town can touch her."

Even Thalia couldn't deny it. "Well, I'll certainly be careful not to," she said offensively. "You realise if we

Langford women boycott her, she'll have very little chance of getting off the ground.''

"What, boycott another Langford enterprise?" Kendall asked cynically.

"My dear girl, what your stepmother is contemplating is so small Nick would scarcely blow his brains out if he had to write the whole thing off. After all, he's an extremely rich man and it was no surprise to us to find out your family haven't even got a cracker.''

"I imagine you felt duty bound to investigate?"

"Precisely,'' Thalia returned cooly. "Father was shocked.''

"To the finger ends,'' Kendall murmured abstractedly. "You certainly don't believe in wasting any time, do you?''

"In your case I decided I'd better not!'' Thalia snapped shortly. "I happen to believe you're hell bent on making a silly little ass of yourself.''

A girl shouldn't have to go through all this, Kendall thought, not on the one day, so she shook her head firmly.

"What nonsense!''

"*Is* it?'' Thalia challenged her bleakly. "I would have thought it was nonsense myself up until the other night. The last time I saw you, you were in white ankle socks with your hair braided, so yo can imagine what a shock I received when I saw you dancing with Nick. Your expression was unmistakable!''

"But fairly normal for any woman enjoying Nick's attention.''

"Hell!'' Thalia burst out explosively, "you're not a woman, you're just a silly kid, a little older than usual for going through your first crush. Why, I've never seen anything so embarrassing in my life!''

"So what?'' Kendall returned laconically. "Nick can conclude I'm just dumb.''

"You're something else as well,'' Thalia told her

scathingly, "you're an opportunist like your step-mother!"

Kendall saw red. It was all too easy for her these days. "Pity you didn't think of it yourself," she said explosively. "It must be a crashing bore sitting around the house all day."

"Why, the *nerve*!" A trace of shock crossed Thalia's aristocratic face. No one had ever challenged her before about her leisurely way of life. "If it's one thing I can't endure it's upstarts!"

"Exactly what *I* think," Kendall said smoothly. "Now I'd like to point out that Nick is coming back."

On the instant Thalia straightened and her grim expression gave way to a warm, strangely vulnerable smile. "Hi, cousin! I've just been enjoying a little chat with Kendall."

"Then you know her father has been taken ill?" Nick glanced briefly from one girl to the other.

"Why...er...no!" Thalia immediately turned back to Kendall. "You never told me."

"I didn't want to spoil your evening," Kendall said evenly. "Surely you're not alone?" It was a trace of pure feline malice, for Kendall had already spotted Thalia's date.

"Actually I'm having dinner with Dean," Thalia explained to Nick almost apologetically.

"Oh?" Nick's eyebrows rose fractionally. "How very interesting."

"He's not bad company," Thalia said abruptly.

"All right, then. Take it easy," said Nick. "I haven't seen that dress before."

"Do you like it?" The way she looked, the way she said it made Kendall realise what Dean Hallitt had told her was true. Thalia was hopelessly in love with her own cousin.

"It's very eye-catching!" Nick sounded genuinely admiring. "Hallitt's making no move to get out of his car, so I suppose we'd better let you go."

"Yes." Thalia still had her face tilted up to Nick. She was a tall woman, but as she had once told her mother, Nick always made her feel small and dainty. "We're seeing you tomorrow night, aren't we?"

"Sure," Nick answered economically.

"We all so enjoy your company." Thalia laughed gaily. "Goodnight, Kendall. I do hope your father gets better."

"Goodnight." For the life of her Kendall couldn't respond to the so-ungenuine friendliness. It was so depressing seeing Thalia's eyes grow big and soft and glimmering, and she began to wonder if Nick had given her good reason. Her own heart felt like a dead weight and she was anxious to get the prescription back to her father.

"Why the blazes she bothers with Hallitt, I don't know," said Nick as they made a right-hand turn out of town.

"Since she can't have you I suppose anyone will do," Kendall replied shortly.

"What the devil are you talking about?" Nick threw her an irritated look.

"Think about it," Kendall said with mock amiability.

"You surely don't think her feelings for me are more than cousinly?"

"I'm quite certain they're not," said Kendall, "and so are you. Personally I'm against too close blood relationships."

"On what grounds?" His black eyes just glanced on her. "Moral, genetic, what? It would be quite legal for me to marry Thalia and we could have a big church wedding as well."

"Then try not to keep her waiting," she said, matching his mocking, sarcastic tone, "if you want to produce the miracle baby, your son and heir."

"I think you'd better sit still and be quiet," Nick told her. "I know you find it hard, but I'll retaliate if you don't."

"Oh really, *how*?"

For answer he pulled the car off the road, put it in Park, reached a hand out for her and kissed her mouth hard. "That's *how*."

"I *loathe* you," she said shakily, when she could speak. She did too, because he knew he could destroy her.

"Keep it up and I'll give you good cause." His eyes gleamed, narrowed and ruthless, and his hand twined rather cruelly through a thick swathe of her hair.

Excitement and anger was all twisted up inside her and she moaned: "Let me go, Nick!"

"Because you can't deal with this?" he asked tightly.

"No, I *can't*!" She shouted it, because it was so humiliatingly true. It was frightening the way her body responded to him, everything moving too violently, too fast, putting too much pressure on her.

"The truth is, you're frightened of an adult situation," he said tersely, "that's why you spend so much time with Hogan."

The thought seared her because it might have been true. "Leave Colin out of this!" she said wearily, still feeling Nick's kiss on her mouth. "All I want is a friend, not a lover."

"Okay." He released her abruptly and turned away, his jaw set. "You're looking at the best friend you've got."

CHAPTER SIX

THE premises Nick selected for Pamela's boutique were excellent and consequently expensive to lease, but it was obvious to Kendall that Pamela had never felt so satisfied in her life. Over the past month her marriage had settled down and the creative fulfillment she had searched for without knowing was supplied by this, her new career.

At Nick's insistence, Kendall had given up her job at the mill, and was to all intents and purposes Pamela's valuable right hand. There was so much to be done; so many trips, so much buying. Harry had to take over the responsibility of supervising the shop. An interior design firm had been called in to make the necessary renovations and supply the furnishings, but Harry always met them each morning at the door, occasionally offering brilliant suggestions, but more often than not getting in the way.

Of course the word had spread like wildfire. Everyone for hundreds of miles around knew about Pamela Reardon's new venture and Nick Langford's involvement, and a gratifying amount of interest had already been shown. But interest didn't necessarily guarantee that the boutique would be heavily patronised, and Kendall asked bluntly why Pamela couldn't cater for the less affluent set as well. Plenty of her own friends and the women she had worked with at the mill had rung her, happy to think at long last, someone as terrific looking as Pamela was going to be able to help them with dashing, affordable clothes.

This wasn't her intention, but Kendall, knowing her stepmother well, put it as a challenge.

"If they can't learn from you, who are they going to learn from?" she asked winningly.

"Don't push me." Pamela sat at the beautiful French bureau that Nick had so generously lent the shop and pondered. She had started smoking again, no matter what damage she was doing to her lungs, and as a result had lost a quick ten pounds. "You know perfectly well your age range haven't got any money and it's impossible to buy quality cheaply."

"Why don't you get garments made up to your own design?" Kendall suggested. "You've got real style and you know all about figure faults. Surely if you had your own workroom it would cut costs. All of my girl friends are sick of walking around in ordinary old sundresses. You could design something for us, a whole range of summer gear, seeing we hardly have a winter, and believe me, it would take off."

"And it could be very lucrative." Pamela leaned back and crossed her long, shapely legs. "Where would we find women good enough to make up my ideas?"

"Put an ad in the paper," said Kendall. "Many women in the district sew absolutely beautifully, but they don't know about fabrics and patterns and the latest fashions. Besides, you'd be offering them jobs and helping them to a creative outlet as well."

Pamela shrugged. "Leave it alone for the time being. I've got enough on my hands at the moment."

"Sure, boss-lady!" Kendall smiled. "Challenge must be exciting to you. I've never seen you look better."

"Do you really think so?" Pamela looked pleased. "Harry told me the same thing this morning."

"Well, that settles it!" Kendall said gently, and walked to the door. "I'd better go and make those phone calls. Nick thinks we should have a champagne opening, all free."

"I'm terrified about it," Pamela confided, looking as though she had never found herself in such a position in her life.

"You'll handle it," Kendall assured. "I'm sure in my own mind, this is going to be a great success. Especially if you look after us young'uns!"

"It could put a whole lot of noses out of joint," Pamela mused suddenly. "The thought has to be faced."

"Obviously." Kendall turned round and looked at her stepmother. "But that's business. None of the other boutique owners have been exactly straining themselves to look after their customers. Don't have any worries about making them pull up their socks. Competition is supposed to be healthy."

"All right," Pamela laughed. "Don't just stand there! If we're going to be a glittering success you'd better get on the phone. And incidentally," she added with unfamiliar warmth, "you sound great when you're dealing with people. The best P.R. I could get."

"Gee, thanks." Kendall ducked her head modestly. She didn't sound so great when she was talking to Nick, but Pamela was revelling in the situation so much she hadn't noticed.

Colin picked her up that evening with the rain streaming down the windscreen and car windows.

"Boy, I hope that cyclone veers away," Colin said worriedly. It was the season for cyclones and one was lashing the Far North, making its presence felt for miles along the coast.

"It was stationary the last time I heard." Kendall leaned forward and wiped over the windscreen with a cloth from the glove box. Rain and steam seemed to be swirling everywhere.

"If we get any flood rains, I'll be in a hell of a mess," Colin said gloomily. "These cyclones are so destructive, aren't they?"

"A fact of life for our world." Kendall spoke calmly, trying to soothe him. Colin had told her a cyclone had almost devastated their farm when he had been a boy; lifting the roof off, smashing windows and ruining the floor coverings and curtains and furniture, with flood waters inundating their land.

"I bet Nick's praying it holds off as well. I'm going to the sale, you know." Colin was speaking loudly against the drumming of the rain.

Kendall said nothing, implying by her silence she wasn't greatly interested in one of Flamingo Park's famous sales.

"How's the business going?" Colin tried a new tack. "I hardly ever see you these days. You've changed."

"Changed?" Now he had her full attention. "In what way?"

"Well, you dress up more." Once started Colin was going to finish. "You don't look like the old Kendall at all. I mean, I always knew you were beautiful, but now it's sort of made you unapproachable; make-up, the new hair-style, the latest gear."

"You don't like it?" Kendall asked him, feeling a little sad.

"No." Colin shook his head. "I suppose before, I thought I had a chance, but now you look so damned classy you don't look at all the sort of person who would be happy on a farm."

"What rot!" Kendall protested violently. "Can't you see through to *me*, the real person, or are you going to be intimidated by a few fancy clothes?"

"Don't be angry!" Gently Colin covered her hand with his own. "Try to understand how I feel. I love you, Kendall. It's getting worse instead of better."

"*Don't*, Colin," she begged.

"I know," he squeezed her hand. "It's pointless, isn't it?"

"I've never promised you any more than my friendship."

"But I didn't want to believe it, you see," Colin continued to hold her hand tightly when he should have had two hands on the wheel. "What do you really see in me, Kendall? Tell me, I want to know."

"I see you as my very good friend," she said, trying to humour him. "A person I can be comfortable with."

"Comfortable—*God*!" Colin swore. "You don't imagine that's how I feel about you?"

"I didn't think you felt very intensely at all," she said quietly. "About me, I mean."

"Mother thinks you're just using me. Too often. A safe refuge when you feel like getting out of the house."

"How cruel!" Kendall was shocked. "To you as well as me."

"It seems to me she has a point," Colin dug in. "You're the prettiest girl in the whole damn town, yet you have a shining reputation. Most of the fellows aren't even game to ask you out, or they know it's no go. You've been tantalising us all for years, yet you don't seem to want any action."

"Action as in sleep around?" Kendall jerked her hand away angrily. "Is that what you're getting at?"

"As a matter of fact I am!" Colin said bitterly, still smarting from an unheard-of argument he had had with his mother. "Maybe you miss out on something vital. Even Sue let me kiss her a lot longer and deeper than you ever would."

Kendall jerked in her seat and stared at him. "It just shows how little I understand about passion. Honestly, Colin, I agree with your mother, you'd be much better off sticking with Sue."

Colin shook his head. "Shut up," he said harshly. "I only kissed her anyway to try and free myself of my obsession with you."

"What a risky thing to do! You could hurt her badly."

"And it didn't work!" Colin said in that same, flat, hard tone. "Sue's a nice girl, a sweet girl, but she does nothing for me."

The unaccustomed violence of his thoughts was colouring his driving. The car was moving too swiftly in the heavy rain and sharp stones were hitting against the paintwork. It was very unpleasant and Kendall was reminded vividly of her recent accident.

"Slow down," she said sharply. "It's not sensible to speed along in the rain."

Colin couldn't get his foot off the accelerator. Normally so calm and collected as he was, the argument with his mother had set him off. A fierce anger blazed hotly inside him, a frustration. He had been Kendall's shadow for years, devoted to her, always on hand. But it couldn't go on for ever. He wanted more. There was only one thing he hadn't tried—overpowering her, making love to her until he had her clinging to him. Of course she thought he didn't have the nerve. So cool, so chaste—beautiful, tormenting Kendall.

He swung off the road so abruptly Kendall was startled into a tiny scream. "What on earth are you doing?"

"What I should have done before!" He switched off the engine and rather clumsily lurched over in her direction.

"Oh, hell!" Kendall sounded more disgusted than frightened, and it added fuel to the fire.

"Kiss me," he demanded thickly, and laced his hand through her hair.

"Why the blazes should I?" Kendall asked angrily. "If you're not careful, we'll be bogged down here for the night."

"Great!" Colin laughed rather wildly. "It's about time I did something mad."

"Oh, please stop," Kendall begged, feeling saddened

and ill. "Come on, Colin, start the car up again before we're feet deep in mud."

Colin shook his head. "I can't go on like this, Kendall."

"I'm sorry, I'm *very* sorry." She was trying to comfort him. She didn't know why.

"No, you're not!" Colin stated emphatically. "Mother said you know perfectly well you've been leading me on."

"And of course you have to line yourself up with Mother."

At this point Colin lost all control. He tightened his hold on her violently and sought for her mouth.

"Damn!" Kendall struggled, but this only angered him more.

"Give a little!" he pleaded in a husky, little-boy tone.

"This is heaven, I'm sure!" She had a crick in her neck and he was almost cutting off her wind.

He still held her tightly, raining kisses all over her unprotected face. "You really want to let go, but you can't. Obviously the whole thing goes back to your childhood."

"Oh, you idiot!" Using all her strength, she pushed at him violently. "Will you stop quoting your crazy mother!"

"She's right about you," said Colin, looking directly into her eyes. "You just haven't developed in some way. You're scared of involvement."

"I'll handle it when I'm older," Kendall told him with bitter humour. "So far, all that's wrong with me is I won't let you or your mother press me into an early marriage."

"It's what you want." Colin reached for her again, his infatuation beyond his control.

Kendall didn't even ponder the situation. She jerked open the door and got out in the pouring rain.

"Kendall!" She could hear Colin's wail of protest in

the instant before she slammed the door so hard it made the little car rock.

God, she thought, my life's suddenly become unstuck. What was she supposed to do now? She had no intention of putting up with Colin in his present mood even though he too, was out of the car, calling bleatingly:

"Kendall. . .*Kendall*!''

It was lunatic, both of them acting like that. Quickly she moved out of the long grass and on to the gravel. Arguments were unpleasant enough in good weather, but they were terrible out in the rain.

"Kendall, don't be like this!'' Colin called, slithering on the wet grass and just barely righting himself.

The imbecility of it! Kendall kept marching with her head down, determined on making it back to the farm under her own steam.

"Oh, Lord,'' Colin shouted, "come on back! I've hurt my ankle.''

He could have, of course, but somehow she didn't think so. Not seriously anyway. Pamela would be furious when she walked in in her ruined outfit.

The car was a distance off before its headlights picked her up in its glare. The driver must have switched on the main beam to make certain there really was a lunatic out there in the rain, for she instantly registered the brighter, piercing light. The only thing wrong with burning one's barges was, one invariably ended up in a mess.

The car nosed past her slowly, while the driver looked out disbelievingly, then pulled up ahead.

"What are you doing?'' Nick enquired, when she drew alongside.

"Nothing,'' she said brightly.

"You seem to be quite good at it.''

"You should get out yourself and walk around in the rain. It makes a change.''

Colin had limped up to them and he addressed Nick with a good deal of deference and embarrassment rolled into one. "Good evening, Nick!"

"My God, what's wrong with the young people of to-day?" Nick asked no one in particular. "I take it you two have had a fight."

"Not at all!" Kendall made scoffing sounds. "We just had a difference of opinion on how we were going to spend the evening."

"What's wrong with dry?" Before she knew it Nick had swung out of the car and bundled her up. At least he was dressed for the occasion in a dark-coloured rain-coat, though his head was bare.

"No, really, I prefer to walk."

"Suicide in the rain," he said lightly, but almost tossed her in.

There were a few moments while he spoke to Colin, then he was behind the wheel again. "It's quite a job, getting you reared," he commented.

"And you don't get paid for it either."

"Or thanked," he returned bluntly. "God, you're wet!"

"At least I offered to walk." Kendall drew herself into a small huddle.

"I haven't even got a blanket," he lamented, sounding hard and a little impatient. "I'll take you home with me."

"*No . . . no*," she repeated more quietly after the first hysterical outburst. "I'm still having nightmares from the last time."

"Don't flatter yourself it could happen again," he said caustically.

"But it could!" Maddened by her own and Colin's conduct, let alone her dripping state, she felt her flip-pant tongue begin to run away with her. "I've just nominated you as the man I most desire to have my universally-held-to-be-necessary first affair with."

"Then you're not planning it right!" he returned in the same deflating tone.

"You don't think I'd benefit?" she asked with false jauntiness.

"You'd benefit more from being turned over my knee." He took the fork that led to the crater road.

"Oh, Nick!" she sighed.

"What's the matter?" he asked quietly.

"Nothing. Everything, I guess." She had tucked her skirt so closely around her it resembled a bandage. "Lord, this is a quiet car!"

"Forget the car, we're talking about you."

"You're simply too good to me at times." She twisted her hair into a plait.

"And it's not easy!" Nick threw her a concerned glance. "I always said you reminded me of a siren, but I didn't mean you to keep getting wet."

"I'm all right, but I feel a pang for the car." She slumped back into the leather seat. "I never knew Colin felt as strongly about me as he does. Do you find that difficult to understand?"

"Not in the least," he said crisply. "You simply haven't considered him at all."

"Well, I *did* ask." She gave a little gasp of pain.

"You've been so actively involved in looking after your father, trying to make ends meet, you don't see things that should be very obvious to you," he told her. "The time's come to set young Hogan free. He's developing quite a fixation."

"So I don't talk to him any more. Not tomorrow when he rings to say he's sorry. Not ever."

"Sooner or later he'll get the message," Nick replied laconically. "The decision has to be made. Don't you agree?"

"Poor Colin!" She heaved a miserable sigh. "Why are we all so set on complicating our lives?"

"Following dreams, I suppose," he said musingly.

"Aren't you even going to ask me how I happened to be on this road tonight, or do you look on me as some sort of guardian angel who hovers around waiting for the right moment?"

"I suppose I do." She looked at him in surprise. "I've got used to it. Remember how you turned up the time I had snakebite?"

"Just as well," he pointed out. "You mightn't be sitting there now."

"Wasn't Harry in a mess! He thought I was going to die."

"I don't see why not. It was possible." He took his eyes off the road fractionally to glance at her. "It's Harry I want to see tonight. I have a couple of Texan buyers coming over for the sale. One of them is mad about horses; paintings, sculptures, in the flesh. Harry paints horses better than anyone I know. . . ."

"And *dust*," said Kendall with a quick surge of delight. "That action painting he did for you of those wild brumbies is terrific!"

"I want to give it to Jake," Nick continued. "There's no time to paint another one now and Jake could be the means of opening up a whole lot of commissions. All cattle men love horses and I know Jake's going to flip over *Stampede*. It's big and it's colourful and full of excitement. It's Harry at his best."

"But he painted it for you," Kendall spoke to him directly. "For you he made the supreme effort. He just went at it until it was finished, then he told us it painted itself."

"He can do it again," Nick said crisply. "It was no accident, no one-off. He can do it and he *will*. But first I want to tell him what I plan to do."

When they arrived back at the farm Nick gave Kendall his raincoat to hide her wet dress. Her hair could be explained away easily, also the fact that Colin was having trouble with his car and thought it better to limp home. Pamela was busy at her desk and Harry accepted the too simple explanation, so Kendall was able to dash away to the shelter of her room.

When she emerged again and walked into the living room, Pamela shot her a sharp glance but said nothing, and Kendall knew the true story would be wrung out of her later. Harry was insisting that Nick should have a drink, thereby hoping to get one himself, but Nick very smoothly declined. He slid expertly into his request while the smile on Harry's face stiffened uneasily.

"I don't think I could do it again," he said finally.

"Of course you could!" Kendall came to sit on the arm of his chair. "You're unbeatable painting horses—you know you are. Rudy told you once you could make a fortune if you just stuck to painting horses."

"Occasionally I like to paint something else," Harry said dryly. "My seascapes are just as good...better!" The blood seemed to have rushed to his face and there was a pulse beating in his temple.

"Naturally, Harry, I wanted to consult you," Nick told him, his black eyes narrow and inscrutable.

"Of course you did." Harry hammered on the side of the chair with his nails. "The truth is, Nick, I don't think I've got it any more. The muse has left me."

"Oh *really*, Harry...." Pamela started in to nag.

"It was just a suggestion," Nick said encouragingly. "No one wants you to whip up something overnight. But I'm a firm believer in your ability, Harry. I imagine every artist or writer goes through a period of self-doubt, then you're out of it. We're all afraid of something."

"Not you, Nick," Harry asserted positively. "I'm the one who's going downhill."

"You've got it in your power to pull up, and don't deny it," Nick told him. "Are you willing for me to sell the painting to Jake? I just know he's going to want it and money no object."

"Well, Nick," Harry gave his friend a long, thoughtful stare, "it won't be easy for me to come up with something as good as *Stampede* again."

"I think you will," Nick stood up and put his hand on Harry's shoulder. "You might make a start painting my new stallion."

"Not Domino?" Surprisingly Harry's voice was unsteady.

"Domino," said Nick. "He might try to savage you if you get too close."

"Don't worry, I'll keep at a safe distance." Harry began to grin, totally absorbed now in some inner idea. "I guess you couldn't fault him for conformation, and there's that magnificent black coat. Like satin."

"Don't ever get too close to him," Nick warned.

"I won't!" Harry nodded a half a dozen times. "Anyway, I'm not afraid of horses. That's it, you see. They always know when you're afraid."

"There's no risk, is there, Nick?" Kendall asked, her mind going back reluctantly to the time one of Nick's colts had overwhelmed the stable boy and badly injured him.

"We'll arrange it that there won't be," Nick answered carelessly, used to horses all his life.

Harry laughed and came to his feet briskly. "You know what this is, don't you? Blackmail."

Nick shook his head. "Domino's the finest stallion I've ever owned. I paid a fortune for him so now I've earned the right to have him painted. By the *best*."

Harry chuckled appreciatively. "You sure know how to get a man to make an effort!"

"Ring Huntley when you want to come over," Nick advised. "I mightn't be always around, but Ray will look after you. He's also the best man with Domino."

"Do stay a little bit longer," Pamela looked at Nick anxiously. "I'll make coffee. It's pouring outside."

"I'd like to, Pamela," he said smoothly, "but I'm

taking a couple of overseas calls tonight. Naturally I expect all three of you to turn up on our big day.''

"We wouldn't miss it for the world!" Harry glanced at his daughter and smiled. "I really hate to mention it, but that was some story you gave me tonight.''

"You know how it is," Nick said tolerantly. "An unexpected squabble.''

"And next thing you know, there's Nick to the rescue." Harry glanced shrewdly from one to the other. "Maybe you ought to stay strictly away from us, Nick, if you want to avoid trouble. And that's all we've been to you one way or the other since we came here.''

"I could never agree with that!" Nick gave his devastatingly attractive smile. "Damn it, if this cyclone doesn't veer away we've got trouble.''

"But it's weakening now, isn't it?" Harry said comfortably, not a good man to take cyclones seriously.

"This time last year a third of our pawpaw plantations were devastated. The laden trees just collapsed in the mud.''

"I remember," said Kendall, her face sober. "Colin is really worried.''

"I'm not sure we're too interested in Colin now," said Harry. "What would have happened if Nick hadn't come along?''

"Well, he *did*.''

"I make a habit of it," Nick confirmed dryly. "Now I really must go. Kendall, you could return my raincoat.''

"Oh, I'm sorry!" She swung round and put her hand on his arm in apology. "I'll get it. I hung it up in the bathroom. It looks simply *enormous*!''

"I suppose it is on an eighteen-year-old girl." He looked amused, the expression of his darkly bronze face indulgent and mocking.

She flung away then with the lightness and speed of a gazelle. They all relied on Nick so much she didn't wonder Thalia Langford was so bitter and resentful. Perhaps she would be the same in Thalia's place.

Two days before Pamela's boutique opened Kendall had a visit from Sue Lockhart. It was lunchtime and Pamela had gone off to have coffee with Paul Rosen, the senior partner in the interior design firm, who had turned very ordinary office premises into an elegant and very luxurious looking fashion boutique.

Sue walked in rather tentatively, but her sweetly rounded face broke into a smile when she saw Kendall emerge from one of the shuttered cubicles.

"Hi there! Are you alone?"

"It's all mine!" Kendall returned the smile. "How's things?"

"Not bad," Sue said a little guardedly. "Daddy's worried about the cyclone, of course. Wouldn't you think it would blow away to sea?"

"Unfortunately they're not so obliging," Kendall pulled out a little giltwood velvet-covered chair and made Sue sit down in it. "Well, what do you think?"

"Very swishy!" Sue looked around with wide eyes. "It must have cost a million dollars."

"It didn't, but it looks it, that's the main thing." Kendall went to sit behind Pamela's exquisite bureau. "Isn't this magnificent?" She rubbed her fingers reverently over the ormolu mountings. "Nick lent it to the shop."

"He's terribly generous, isn't he?" Sue said with no hidden meaning but warm sincerity. "I mean, Daddy says he's put this town on the map almost singlehanded. There's been such a boom ever since we arrived."

"I suppose it all comes from being a human dynamo and setting your goals high," Kendall smiled a little wryly. "What brings you into town today? Doing a little shopping?"

For a moment Sue seemed flustered by the direct

question, and her blue eyes darkened. "Actually, Kendall, I wanted to speak to you about something. Something that's been bothering me."

"Colin?"

"How did you know?"

Kendall's green eyes glowed. "You really like him a lot, don't you?"

"He belongs to you." Sue looked down at her feet, a small blonde girl in a yellow dress.

"You're very much mistaken about that," Kendall said a little impatiently. "Colin and I are friends, Sue, but I do not and will never look on him as anything else."

"But that's not what *he* says!" Sue's creamy skin flamed. "He told me positively he's in love with you."

"He'll get over it," Kendall sighed, thinking herself awful for being totally bored with the subject of Colin. "The point is, I don't love him and I've never given him to understand I did."

"His mother doesn't like you," Sue volunteered a little smugly.

"It doesn't hurt," Kendall said mildly. "But she does like you. You have an ally there."

"I know." Sue nodded emphatically. "I don't know why she doesn't like you. You're terribly popular."

"Thanks," Kendall said dryly. "So far as I'm concerned, Sue, I'd like to see you win Colin around. I mean that sincerely."

"But how do I begin to *do* it?" Sue wailed. "I've thought about it and thought about it and talked it over with Mrs. Hogan...."

"You've *what*?" Kendall was torn by a mad desire to laugh.

"She's been wonderful to me," Sue said earnestly.

"The perfect mother-in-law!"

"Well, they can make or break you." Sue took Kendall's comment seriously. "She thinks I'm absolutely right for Colin."

"I'm pretty impressed myself," said Kendall, thinking of all these private discussions. "But I think you'd both be very wise to appear to allow Colin to make up his own mind."

"Of course." Sue jumped up happily and kissed Kendall on the cheek. "Oh, thank you. I've been *that* worried!"

"You'd have been right to," Kendall said a little tartly, "if Colin and I were as close as you appeared to think."

"But Mrs. Hogan *told* me how you felt!" Sue looked embarrassed. "She really wants the best for him and you're not really that well suited, are you? You're so vivacious and Colin's so gentle, almost shy."

"Well, you know what they say," Kendall said flippantly, "opposites attract."

"I really could *love* him." Sue stood for a moment looking directly into Kendall's green eyes. "Please don't keep his love for you alive."

"Listen, what do you want me to do?" Kendall picked up a paperweight and put it down again, "take a vacation?"

"Be serious, Kendall," Sue said a little sternly. "Forewarned is forearmed. When Colin rings up to ask you out, say you're busy."

"Got it!" Kendall scribbled down the message on the date pad. *"Busy!"* She made a business of underlining the word.

Sighing, Sue gathered up her purse and string bag. "Probably one reason why Mrs. Hogan doesn't like you is the way you seem to turn everything into a joke."

"You're kidding!" Kendall stood up. "Come off it, Sue. Don't turn into another Mrs. Hogan. Not yet."

There were tears in Sue's soft blue eyes. "I'm deadly

serious, Kendall. You've got so many things going for you, let me have Colin.''

"I'll keep my fingers crossed." Kendall matched the action to the words. She felt like crying that Colin wasn't hers to give away. Colin was his own person, not some backward hillbilly who allowed himself to be manipulated by a trio of conniving women.

"I'm really looking forward to the opening," Sue said kindly. "Of course, we could never afford to shop here."

"How do you know?" Kendall sounded pleasantly chiding. "Pamela has all sorts of ideas for various lines. We're not just going to cater to the Country Club crowd. ''We're going to offer style for a reasonable price."

"Oh, great!" Sue didn't look convinced. "I make my own clothes anyway."

"And they're very pretty," Kendall glanced at Sue's little sundress. "But if you really want to knock Colin's eyes out, you'd better get at least a couple of your dresses here."

She smiled again and waved and left Sue on the pavement to mull that one over.

CHAPTER SEVEN

THE weather cleared up miraculously for the opening of the boutique. They had gone over and over chic sounding names for it, but finally Nick suggested keep it simple and stick to the name Pamela had modelled so successfully under—Pamela Paige.

It looked good glittering under the glorious night sky and they had such a crowd there were customers spilling over on to the pavement. A lot of the women had had specially printed invitations sent to them, but although these represented the social elite, Kendall was happy to see the ordinary women of the district taking a great interest.

Pamela had been very clever with her stock and despite the fact the Langford women, Thalia and her mother, had not yet turned up, it looked like being close to a sell-out.

Pamela undoubtedly was the star of the evening. She was splendidly turned out in her favourite white, obviously basking in so much interest and admiration, and she moved from group to group dispensing charm and great dollops of advice that sent the ladies' fingers to their wallets and check books. The champagne, Kendall found, didn't hurt either and they had hired three Italian waiters, all young and good-looking, to be constantly alert and keep up just the right degree of supply.

At twenty to eight—the time on the invitations had stipulated six p.m. to eight p.m.—Thalia and her mother arrived; obviously, from their haughty faces, just to please Nick.

"Why, Mrs. Langford...Thalia!" Pamela swept up to them without gush. "I'm so pleased you could come along."

"Nick asked us." Thalia responded in a flat, carrying tone, her dark eyes ranging with something like distaste over the whole glittering interior and the sea of avidly interested faces.

Mrs. Langford, to her credit, seemed displeased with this studied piece of rudeness, for she apologised very graciously: "I do hope you'll forgive us for being so late."

"No matter!" Pamela dismissed it with a wave of her hand. "Do come in now and see what I've been able to put together. There are some lovely-looking glamour clothes for the evening and a brilliant fire-box red satin that would be perfect for you, Thalia, with your height and strong colouring."

Despite her declared intention of boycotting all Pamela had to offer, Thalia was fairly caught. Although she always thought of herself as totally chic, rich and well traveled, Pamela was one of the few people she had met in her life who made her feel she might be just playing at fashion. Ten pounds and more lighter, made up to the nines, Pamela had it all over her guests psychologically, making them so vulnerable some of them were picking out clothes they simply weren't the right shape for, but there Pamela zoomed in, not even having to work hard to give the right advice.

Kendall, circling the room, saw Mrs. Langford pick up a beautiful black chiffon cardigan beaded in black and silver and not even turn a hair at the price. There was a long black chiffon evening dress to go with it, and it didn't take a moment for Pamela to pull it out and hold it up against her own statuesque figure. Kendall couldn't resist smiling, because it was fairly certain Mrs. Langford was seeing herself in it, being blessed with a tall, lean figure.

At eight o'clock everyone seemed very reluctant to go home, but Pamela considered, very rightly, she had tantalised them long enough. The boutique was open in the morning for five days a week and late night shopping on the Friday, so now they all knew where to come.

It was in the general bustle of departure that the accident occurred. Kendall was holding a very expensive silk crêpe-de-chine dress, about to slip it back on its padded hanger, when one of the women, champagne glass in hand, suddenly lurched into her and spilt the contents of the glass right down the skirt of the model gown.

"Oh dear!" The woman stood there and shook her head looking as if she was about to cry.

"Stay calm." Kendall was dismayed herself, all the more so because her upswept gaze focused on Thalia Langford's carefully arranged face, though she ducked back into the crowd.

"I swear I was *pushed*!" the woman complained.

"Are you serious, Nan?" A friend took the glass out of her nerveless hand.

"Don't worry!" Kendall's smile tried to reassure them both.

"Good heavens, what's happened?" Pamela came up to them, a look of astonishment on her striking face.

"Just a little accident with the wine bottle," Kendall aped a current TV ad.

"I'm *terribly* sorry," the woman, who hadn't bought anything, looked so pale she might have thought Pamela was about to bring charges. "It doesn't alter anything, I know, but I'm quite certain I was pushed from behind. I didn't lose my balance in any way. Someone deliberately knocked into me."

It was apparent from Pamela's expression that her enthusiasm for the evening was about to crack, so Kendall jumped immediately into the breach. "There's always a little bit of chaos on these very *successful* evenings," she glanced meaningfully at Pamela, "think no more about it."

"I'm sure we can get it out easily," Pamela finally managed, staring at the spot. "Now please don't let this spoil your evening," she took her upset guest by the arm, "you must have another glass of champagne before you go home. You too, my dear!" She included the woman's clearly suspicious friend, who seemed inclined to want an investigation.

And she isn't the only one! Kendall thought, looking around again. On the far side of the room, reflected many times in a mirrored alcove, Thalia Langford smiled at her.

Kendall was astounded at how angry she became. Thalia obviously couldn't care less about the damage or upset she had caused. Moreover, she was revelling in the situation, certain she was beyond any form of reprisal. Probably she had been protected all her life, instead of slapped.

Thalia was therefore astounded when Kendall rushed up to her as she was walking to the car.

"That was a pretty miserable thing to do!" Kendall got her hand on the older girl's arm, detaining her.

"Darling—" Mrs. Langford, who had already reached their car, looked back in surprise, alerted by something in both girls' stance.

"You're not going to make a little scene, are you, dear?" Thalia sneered.

"Maybe I've figured out it's what you really need," Kendall said heatedly. "You're just a spoilt-rotten, arrogant bitch!"

"What a lady!"

"Don't *lady* me," Kendall snapped tightly, "ladies don't do what you did and leave an innocent woman to take the blame."

"What is it, girls?" Mrs. Langford came back to them, reluctant to think this could be an argument.

"Nothing." Kendall had had her say and she was ready to stop. After all, Mrs. Langford hadn't done anything except make an awful job of rearing Thalia.

"This cheeky little brat is accusing me of causing that accident to the dress," Thalia told her mother in incredulous tones.

"Surely not?" Mrs. Langford bent a stern gaze on Kendall to make sure she was aware of the seriousness of the charge.

By now Kendall's stomach was turning over and she realised too late that she had created more of a problem with her burst of temper. "I'm prepared to let it go," she said quietly.

"You *believe* it?" Mrs. Langford's eyebrows almost shot to her hairline.

"Obviously she does, or she wouldn't dare stand there," Thalia mocked.

"I don't know if I care for that," said Mrs. Langford.

On the other side of the street, Nick locked his car and came towards them. "Hullo, how did it all go?"

Mrs. Langford pondered an answer, but couldn't seem to find one, and Thalia burst out in a hurt, upset voice. "Badly, I'm afraid. This crazy girl here has just upset Mother and me dreadfully!"

"How?" The street light illuminated Nick's handsome face.

"Please forget it, darling." Mrs. Langford said regally. "I'm sure Nick doesn't want to become involved."

"Well, I am." Nick turned to his aunt by marriage. "I thought I was taking you all out to dinner afterwards?"

"And we were looking forward to it, dear. So *much*!" Mrs. Langford put a heavily jewelled hand to her temple as though a pounding head was starting there.

"What's the trouble, Kendall?" Nick turned to Kendall, who was standing very quietly by his shoulder.

"I'm afraid I wasn't exactly very bright about something."

"I should say *not*!" Mrs. Langford made a sound that was almost a snort. "I insist you apologise."

"Fine," said Kendall. "I apologise. It's a shame, but I will."

"What on earth is she talking about?" Mrs. Langford asked Nick rather faintly.

"Don't let's discuss it here on the footpath," Nick suggested smoothly. "If you like to drive out to the Club, we'll meet you there."

"Not me!" said Kendall, poker-faced.

"Let's go, Mother!" Thalia took her perplexed parent by the arm. "Some people just don't know how to behave."

"Some don't even try!" Kendall's quick tongue couldn't ignore that.

"We'll see you at the Club, shall we, Nick?" Mrs. Langford was obviously loathing every minute.

"Yes, I won't be long." He walked them both to their car, leaned down to say something to his aunt, then returned to Kendall, who seemed rooted to the spot. Pamela would be furious with her for thoroughly antagonising two of the most influential women in the town—*and* prospective good customers in Pamela's view.

Suddenly she was tired, tired of everything and everyone. The evening had started out so excitingly, she looked better than she had ever looked in her life, and the boutique seemed launched on a dazzling success. Now this. Naturally, Nick would be on the side of the beautiful people—his own relatives.

"Listen, little one, you move too fast!" he said to her, confirming it.

"You might be right!" She gave a funny little spurt of laughter. "Pamela will kill me."

"I still don't know what happened." Nick drew her off the sidewalk on to the grassy verge.

"And I don't know how to tell you," she said sarcastically, "considering it involves your beloved cousin."

"Try," he said crisply, "and cut out the wisecracks."

"All right!" She assumed the calm, deliberate tone of a newsreader. "I was putting one of the model gowns away, about three-hundred-and-fifty dollars, when a woman lurched into me and spilt a whole glassful of champagne down the skirt. She swore she was pushed and I know perfectly well who pushed her. I won't mention names."

"It seems you already have," he pointed out very dryly. "Did you actually see Thalia do it?"

"No, I didn't."

"You just *think* she did it. A woman's intuition?"

"Don't knock it," she said sharply. "She did it all right. She even had the hide to smirk."

"At which point you saw red?"

"You know me," she said wryly, and one of the spaghetti straps on her delightful pearly green shift fell off her shoulder. "I go around collecting trouble."

"It would seem like it," Nick was forced to agree.

"So what do I do now? Face the music?"

"Well, I don't think Pamela is going to say you acted admirably." He glanced down at her, the moonlight changing her golden skin to pearl.

"I know—control."

He didn't answer immediately. "For that matter, why should you? I'm only trying to be fair. You're absolutely certain Thalia was responsible?"

"God knows why she did it!" Kendall didn't even bother answering directly. "Who would want to ruin something beautiful?"

"Like my friendship with you?" He put out his hand and tilted her chin up.

"We're not friends," she said solemnly, and her lips trembled.

"No." His fingers were still under her chin and he brushed one lightly across her mouth. "It was my intention to take you all out to celebrate and I don't intend to change it."

"I'd choke!" she exclaimed passionately, and twisted her head away.

"You'd be very unlucky to do that." He took her hand forcibly. "Now we won't spoil Pamela's big evening by telling her any of this. Harry should be here in a minute and we'll all go on to the Club. It's all arranged."

"I tell you I *won't*!" she said mulishly.

"Why, lost your nerve?" He held her hard by his side.

"Not a chance." She had to smile.

"Then come. I promise you Thalia won't bother you. Besides, we have to make up the numbers. There'll be ten of us in all. I've asked along Ian and Susan McEwan and the Jamiesons."

"Yes, I know. They were here tonight."

"So that's settled," he said lightly. "I'll seat you safely away from Thalia."

And from yourself, she thought, but didn't say. They had slaved for weeks on Pamela's new venture and she had come close to undoing all they had achieved with one stupid mistake. People like Thalia Langford were born to go through life doing exactly as they pleased, and all she could do about it was drop the matter fast.

No sooner did cyclone Martha blow out than cyclone Nora blew in, roaring on to the Far Northern Queensland coast and making its presence felt for hundreds of miles along the coast. On the morning of Flamingo Park's annual sale, there was a strong wind blowing and intermittent rain, but it didn't seem to dampen anyone's enthusiasm in the least. This was as much a gala day as one of the top cattle sales in the country and it was the Langford custom to offer a superb barbecue luncheon free.

When Kendall arrived with her father, the very first people she saw were Mrs. Hogan and Colin.

"Dear heaven!" Harry exclaimed, beamed and waved like a hypocrite and made himself scarce.

"Kendall!" Colin was shouting, clearly wanting her to stop.

She could feel herself growing angry at the expression on Mrs. Hogan's face, but she didn't have it in her heart to hurt Colin. He had been her good friend for years.

"Hi!" She gave him a lovely, luminous smile, which of course he took as encouragement.

"Oh, it's good to see you!" His brown eyes shone. "Mother, here's Kendall," he called, like a perfect fool.

"How are you, Kendall?" There was a different light in Mrs. Hogan's eyes.

"Fine, thank you—and you?"

"I'm sorry to say I have a headache."

"It's the weather for it," Kendall tried to remember the times Mrs. Hogan had been nice to her.

"You'll sit with us, won't you?" Colin took her arm, drinking in her appearance like a man long deprived.

"Actually I'm sitting with Harry." Where *was* he, the traitor!

"That's all right, then," Colin smiled. "We can all sit together."

"I'm quite sure Kendall wants to run along," Mrs. Hogan told her son a little sharply.

"You don't, do you, Kendall?" Colin searched her face so forlornly her heart twisted in sympathy.

"I'm quite happy to sit with you," she said evenly, regretting that he should ever have fallen in love with her and spoilt the calm tenor of their friendship.

"What did I tell you?" Colin seemed determined to

ignore his mother's telling expression, because he took
both women by the arm. "We'd better hurry if we want
to get good seats. They tell me Nick's arranged a polo
match for late afternoon. It should be exciting. He's a
smashing player."

Across his radiant face, Mrs. Hogan gave Kendall a
look of blazing fury, but mercifully she missed it, for
she was busy searching out Harry in the swarming
crowd. It was typical of Harry, she thought, to charge
off like that. Mrs. Hogan was on his short list of human
beings to avoid and Kendall supposed she couldn't
blame him. Mrs. Hogan entirely lacked humour, and
such a deficiency shocked Harry to the core.

Nearly everyone in the entire district was there. Even
Pamela had consented to come along for an hour later
on, though she had a frantic distaste for anything on
four legs.

"This place is a dream, isn't it?" Colin murmured
raptly, looking all round him and seeing only perfection.

"A great showplace!" Mrs. Hogan agreed stiffly, as
Colin set a cushion down for her on the white timber
seat.

"A funny thing about cattlemen, they never seem to
get tired of looking at cattle," Colin continued excited-
ly.

"Nick told me it's the only way to learn." Kendall
sank down on Colin's other side. "They study every
beast they see, so they finish up with a keen eye."

"I see Nick's got his American guests with him,"
Mrs. Hogan lost a little of her belligerence as she caught
sight of Nick's party.

"They look *loaded*!" Colin whistled under his
breath.

"They must be, to come all the way from the States,"
Mrs. Hogan said, and began to wave at someone en-
thusiastically.

Both Colin and Kendall turned their heads to see the object of Mrs. Hogan's bottomless pleasure and there was Sue Lockhart looking very pretty in a pink sleeveless dress with a wide-brimmed, pink-ribboned straw hat on her head.

"Move up, Kendall," Mrs. Hogan said briskly. "Here's Sue!"

"Damn it, Mother," Colin hissed angrily. "Didn't I tell you I choose my own friends?"

"Shush!" Kendall pressed her elbow hard into his side. Sue was almost on them and Kendall didn't want to see that tremulous smile wiped off her face. She moved along the bench and patted the place beside her invitingly. In ten minutes the sale would start and later she would find some excuse to move around to the other side of the ring.

As it happened the area around the show ring became so crowded she couldn't have moved, much as she wanted to. Sue was glancing across her so constantly at Colin she would have offered to shift only she feared some outburst from Colin, while on Colin's other side, Mrs. Hogan was almost reduced to facial contortions smiling at Sue and glowering at Kendall. Far away to their left she could see Harry plainly. He had his sketchbook on his knee, busily recording anything and everything that took his fancy. Harry was marvellous at lightning sketches and she knew perfectly well he had forgotten her.

At the lunch break she tried desperately to make her escape. If she could just fight her way around to Harry she would sit quietly under his wing.

"You'll excuse me, won't you?" She smiled at all of them and saw the dawning relief in Sue's china blue eyes. "I think I'll go and join Harry."

"You're coming back, aren't you?" Colin looked as though he was about to forcibly detain her.

"We'll see!" She stood up and smiled at him. "Pamela should be here this afternoon."

"Well then, you'll all want to be together?" At long last Mrs. Hogan dredged up a smile. "I think it very unusual, dear, the way you call your father by his Christian name."

"He likes it," Kendall explained. "It makes him feel young."

"I think he should keep away from those bulls," Colin suddenly said abruptly. "They can be dangerous."

"Yes," Mrs. Hogan let her eyes focus on the yard. "It doesn't do to wander around making sketches."

"I'll tell him." It was Kendall's chance and she took it, almost racing down the tiered rows of seats.

She had her head down watching where she was going when Lot 25 suddenly charged without warning. Women screamed and there was an uproar of sound as an enormous dehorned bull knocked a man to the ground and began to butt him.

It was Harry, and Kendall found herself tearing into the danger zone, mindful of nothing except that her father was down and exposed to serious injury.

"Kendall!" She heard her name shouted, but she was too frantic to stop. Stockmen had converged on the beast, but they didn't seem able to beat it away.

It must have caught sight of her out of the corner of its eye, for it wheeled in a fury and charged her small, flying figure.

Her heart nearly stopped in panic. She had discovered the worst possible way of saving Harry; a victim of her own headlong flight. She made a shuddering effort to alter her course, but now her legs didn't seem to be functioning properly and her heart was leaping out of her breast. She was about to be trampled by a three-hundred-and-fifty-kilogram bull, and death or serious injury was very near.

She opened her mouth to scream, horribly fascinated that no sound came out, but someone caught her up, carrying her off in a desperate running lunge, his strength so bruising the breath was almost knocked out of her and she gave a choking gasp.

For a moment they were both in enormous danger and it was a terrifying sight for the hundreds of shocked onlookers who sighed in relief as they slammed into the fence, the man taking the full force of impact so the sound of his head and his shoulders cracking against the wood was quite audible.

Dead silence now, and Kendall opened her eyes dazed and shocked. Her rescuer was standing over her, still with his arms around her in that crushing lock, a thick runnel of blood running from high above his temple down the lean brown line of his cheek.

"Oh, Nick!" she cried despairingly. In that moment of piercing awareness she knew she would love him until the day she died.

His beautiful shirt was wet with blood, also her bare shoulder and the left side of the tiny bodice of her sundress.

"Oh, Nick!" she whispered again, so weak she would have fallen without his support.

Harry, who had started it all, was now on his feet, shaken and bruised but otherwise unhurt, and at least a dozen stockmen had the bull overpowered, a rope thrown around his massive neck.

"My God, Nick!" Harry limped up to them. "Are you all right?"

"Mr. Langford?" Nick's manager was there and a wavering circle of anxious faces.

"Get the bull back into the yard," said Nick curtly.

"Yes, sir. Right away."

She felt as if she was sinking into some black fog, a sickness in the pit of her stomach.

"Don't faint!" Nick ordered so firmly above her, she found herself straightening.

Dr. Richardson was there, looking a little grey, and he spoke gravely to Nick. "You'd both better come up to the house for a while. I'd better take a look at that head injury."

"I'm all right!" Nick grimaced and looked down at himself and Kendall. "It looks a lot worse than it is."

"You were lucky!" said Harry in heartfelt tones. "God, why didn't you let the bull butt *me* a few times? I'd die rather than have either of you injured!"

"Settle down, Harry." Nick looked into Harry's distressed face, seeing his high colour. "You'd better come up to the house with us. I'll need to change this shirt."

It was Kendall's intention to walk by herself, and she even made a serious attempt to free herself but then the frightening dizziness came back and she slumped forward harmlessly into Nick's arms.

NICK himself came back to the house a few hours later to check on her and found her coming out of a mildly sedated sleep.

"All right?" He sat on the side of the bed and looked down into her face. She had lost that deathly paleness; her black silky hair tumbled about her sleep flushed face and her unguarded eyes were a deep, glittering green.

"How am I ever going to be able to thank you, Nick?" she whispered.

"I'll think of something," he said lightly.

"*Tell* me." She sat up suddenly, grasped his wide shoulders and searched his dark face. "I think I'd be dead, except for you."

"Forget it," he said a little harshly.

"I *can't*!" Her voice was muffled and shaky. "Even when I was asleep I was dreaming. Poor Harry, he was so shocked at what he did."

Nick gave a faint laugh, drew her towards him and

cradled her head. "Strangely enough he's over it now. What I call Harry showing the reverse side of the coin. He and Jake are enjoying themselves enormously."

"Harry always does mad things when there's a wind blowing," she offered solemnly. "It's a wonder we all came out of it as well as we did. How's your head?" She lifted her face to him, her green gaze so intense she might have been searching for the very essence of him.

"No problem." Carelessly he dismissed a few stitches.

"How little you make of it!" she accused him almost mournfully and, lost to her impulses, drew his head down and kissed the polished, rasping, smoothness of his cheek. "Thank you, Nick, for everything."

It was a curious moment, one of electric tension, and she felt the coiled reaction in his lean, powerful body.

"Is that the best you can do?" he asked dryly, and his hands tightened on her waist.

"That's all I can manage for right now." Despite the answering tension she felt in him, there was nothing to learn from his face but a hard, mocking challenge.

"*Is* it?" He pushed the heavy hair back from her face and in a spontaneous, uncontrolled gesture she turned her cheek into his palm.

"Don't hurt me, Nick." All her nerves were flaring in a riot, yet she spoke with helpless trust.

"You little fool!" In a blind moment he moved her steadily towards him so she was half lying in his arms.

"I *can't*...." The tears were gathering in her tight throat, but she had to speak before he overwhelmed her.

"Isn't there a little resistance in all loving?" he asked huskily, his eyes on her young, transparent face.

"*Nick.*" His words seemed to set her on fire, tightening the excitement until it spilled everywhere.

"I won't hurt you, I promise."

With exquisite tenderness his mouth moved across her wet cheek, trailed to the corner of her trembling mouth,

then closed on its cushioned softness with such passion
she had the dazzling sensation that lightning had split
her asunder.

The fruit of the tree of knowledge, was it bitter or
sweet?

The broken little whimper was her own, then exulta-
tion replaced the pain. She felt Nick's hand move to her
breast, cupping it possessively, soaring her hunger, so
she was faced with the shattering realisation that behind
her unsullied innocence was a very passionate woman
craving satisfaction.

The thought was too much and she twisted in his
arms, her eyes tightly closed in ecstasy and fear.

"Don't Nick. Please don't!"

She begged him in vain, or he didn't even hear her,
because he turned her back to him again and kissed all
the way down her throat to the cleft between her
breasts. It made her extremely excited, the desperate
need and the want. It was a near craziness to want as
much as this....

She cried out again, frustrated little moans, and he
stemmed the impassioned sounds with his mouth.

Instantly she fought him, awed by the intensity of her
own emotions, the terrible risks involved in playing with
fire, but he held her implacably, one moment so tender,
the next, so obviously her master.

"Open your mouth, Kendall," he murmured tautly.

She shook her head, almost violently angry with the
burden of loving.

"Don't you want to?" He leaned back a little and
looked down at her, eyes and mouth tightly closed.
She looked beautiful, a little wild, with a pulse beating
madly at the base of her throat. "Kendall?" He traced
the outline of her lips with his fingertip until her eyelids
fluttered and finally she had to look at him.

"You're the cool one, Nick," she whispered helplessly. "I'm frightened."

"I know it." He bent his dark head and kissed the fluttering pulse in her throat.

"You can't know!" Her body arched instinctively as though it belonged to him. "How can you know how I feel? You're a man, experienced and secure. You say you don't want to hurt me, but I'm frightened you're going to do just that."

"You mean you're terrified of letting yourself go. The person you're really frightened of, Kendall, is yourself."

"And if I am?" Her eyes filled with tears. "Does that mean I have to make you a gift of myself?"

"It seems to me you'd be glad to," he said bluntly, and tightened his hold on her.

"You *demon*!" She literally saw red.

"No Kendall, don't!" He pinned her wrists. "You need this. I know it's painful, but I won't lose control."

She was too far gone now to care what he did, but when he saw her resistance was finished he slackened his iron hold on her and she seemed to dissolve right into his arms.

Why had she ever bothered to fight him when she wanted this so badly? Her fears dropped away, and her will, and she allowed him to kiss her so deeply even his resolve seemed swept away in the turbulent flow of emotion.

They were falling together back on the bed, when a woman's voice screamed insanely from the doorway.

"Nick!"

Reality came back in an instant. Kendall fell against the pile of heaped-up pillows, but Nick turned back unselfconsciously. "That's a hell of a way to get my attention!"

Thalia slammed the door shut and stood there staring at them with her jaw fallen in shock. "What are you doing?" she cried accusingly.

"What a question!" Nick shrugged his broad shoulders and stood up. "Does it bother you?" he asked bluntly.

"Yes, it does." She took a step towards him as though unsure whether to spring at his throat or fall at his knees. "You surely have no interest in this child?"

"That's absolutely none of your business," he returned evenly.

"Be fair, Nick, it *is*!" Thalia's body was shaking, even her voice. "Why, she nearly got you killed this morning!"

"Nonsense!" Nick dismissed that with a wave of his hand. "Is there something you want, Thalia?"

"God, you're cruel, Nick!" she said brokenly, and raised her clenched fist to her working mouth.

"Just a minute, please!" Kendall thrust her legs over the side of the bed and stood up rather groggily. "I don't want to hear this."

"I'd prefer you stay in bed," Nick said firmly.

"So why don't you carry her off to *your* bedroom?" Thalia screeched. "Just another conquest for the almighty Nick!"

"Strangely enough," Nick said mildly, "conquests don't interest me in the least."

"No, it all comes too damned easy!" Thalia's dark eyes rested on her cousin with the unmistakable look of anger and burning jealousy. Round spots of colour stood out on her strong cheekbones and she looked so sick and distressed Kendall's too tender heart began to ache for her.

"Might I be excused from this little scene?" She tried standing up again, though she had shrunk back from Nick the last time.

"You conniving little bitch!" Thalia leaped towards her like a snake about to strike.

"Stop that!" Nick reached out and gave Thalia a tap on her unprepared cheek. "Kendall is pretty unusual in that regard."

"Not from what I saw!" Thalia cried. "What are you trying to do to me, Nick? I've loved you all my life!"

"How terrible!" Kendall whispered with real sympathy, and gave Nick a hard stare. "Why don't you put her out of her misery?"

"If I knew exactly what it was," he said, looking all at once terribly bored.

"She loves you. You *must* know!" Kendall stopped in front of him, swaying a little dizzily.

"I could name you nearly thirty women who've told me that," Nick said disagreeably, and put a steadying hand on her shoulder.

"You *enjoy* it!" she accused.

"Indeed I don't," he said crisply. "But it's easy attracting women when you're a millionaire."

"It's you," Thalia said piteously, "not your money."

"Oh?" Nick's black eyes sparkled ironically. "Life wouldn't be too wonderful for you in a cottage. In any case, you're talking nonsense. I've never acted any way towards you but properly."

"But it's always been understood. . . ." Thalia sank into an armchair, her eyes clinging to him.

"What has?" he asked politely.

"You know damned well," said Kendall, trying vainly to brush his hand away.

"Will you *shut up*!" He gave her a sharp downward glance.

"No, I won't!" she cried, coming straight to the point. "Even *I* heard there was going to be an engagement!"

"For God's sake," muttered Nick, "is it any wonder I stay away from women?"

"Nevertheless they don't stay away from *you*," Kendall countered bluntly. "Either you're going to get engaged to her or you're *not*!"

For answer he lifted her very deliberately and plonked her down on the bed. "Sit still and mind your own business," he said briskly, then turned to his cousin, his handsome dark face alive with sarcasm. "You must really be in love, Thalia. You haven't said a word for ten minutes."

"I love you, Nick," she breathed with her head down.

"Then you need treatment," he told her shortly.

"Hell, that's a cruel thing to say," Kendall called loudly. "I mean, which psychiatrist does she see?"

"Pretty soon, Kendall, I'll beat you," Nick turned on her like no gentleman. "Just leave it alone."

"Thalia has a problem—you can see that."

Thalia *was* slumped in the chair, leaning over like a woman in pain.

"Are you suggesting I don't leave her out on a limb and marry her?" Nick asked with black amusement.

"You've got to marry someone!" Thalia threw up her head bravely.

"Right at this moment there's nothing I'd like better than to toss you two out!" Nick's white teeth snapped in irritation and Kendall jumped up, the pupils of her eyes dilating so the black invaded the green. She felt faintly giddy, but that didn't matter in the least.

"I'll show you there's one you don't have to toss out!" she cried in a fierce little voice.

"Good for you," Thalia said applaudingly, obviously intent on staying, only Nick got a hand under her arm and lifted her out of the chair.

"Out!" he ordered, his voice so dangerously emphatic that she capitulated suddenly and moved to the door. "Get back into bed, Kendall." He turned a granite profile.

"That's right—worry about *her*!" Thalia's scarlet mouth worked in distress. "I've given you my life, yet you owe *me* nothing!" Humiliated tears sprang to her eyes and she turned on her heel and dashed away.

"How sad!" For a few seconds Kendall thought she was about to faint again.

"Damn it, the last thing I wanted was for her to upset you." A wild kind of anger prowled in Nick's eyes, but he came to her and lifted her gently back into bed.

"But you made love to her, Nick?" She threw him a shimmering, troubled glance.

"If I may be so ungallant, the thought never entered my head." Angry he looked as arrogant as the devil.

"What a hopeless tangle!" she sighed wearily.

"It *would* be if I let women run my life." He looked down at her with brilliant, cold eyes. You're obviously still feeling the effects of the sedative. My advice is, if it means anything at all to you, shut your eyes and go to sleep."

CHAPTER EIGHT

THALIA and her mother, of course, never came to the boutique after that, but although Pamela felt angry and snubbed about it, she had little else to complain of. The word had gone around that Pamela Paige's haute couture collection and the shop was being so heavily patronised by the wives and daughters of the sugar, timber and beef barons, that Pamela found it necessary to fly off on an unscheduled buying trip to the southern capitals, leaving Kendall in charge.

In a way she enjoyed it. Pamela wasn't the easiest person to work for, so it was a pleasant change to be left alone, but such excitements as there were in running a dress shop didn't appeal to Kendall's temperament. She was essentially a very active person, both mentally and physically, and now the real work was over there was far too much standing around. Pamela had made it plain she didn't need her on the buying trips and, of course, someone had to look after the customers.

When she got home that night Harry welcomed her warmly, waving his whisky glass. "I had a call from Pamela," he told her. "She won't be home until the weekend."

"You sound pleased!" Kendall slumped into a chair. It always bewildered her, the way Harry sounded pleased.

"Oh well, darling," Harry tried to shrug off his unhusbandly attitude, "you know how it is. You and I are such pals, it makes a nice change to have Pammy away. Everything is so nice and quiet and normal."

"Oh, Harry!" She didn't know whether to laugh or to cry. "Is that your first Scotch for the night?"

"I'm surprised you asked!" He winked at her without really answering at all. "Can't I get you something, darling, you look a little frazzled."

"I'm all right," she said, knowing full well she didn't look her usual, buoyant self. Colin had called in that afternoon to beg her to come out with him and the whole thing had been rather upsetting.

"I'll get you something anyway," Harry gave her an anxious look, "plenty of soda water and ice."

"I bet you didn't do the laundry?" She got up and walked through to the kitchen.

"We'll start on it after tea."

Kendall smiled and went to the fridge. "Salad and cold meat?" she called.

"Anything." Harry returned with a long, frosty drink. "I've been eating salads until they come out my ears and I haven't lost a pound."

"You're not fooling me, mate," she said firmly.

"Wait until the day *you* have to diet," he pointed out reproachfully. "It's not easy."

"I know it's not. But you're going to do it." She moved quickly and efficiently about the kitchen, humming a song as she worked. A sad little song really, but she wasn't aware of it.

"Was it awful, the shop?" Harry sat down happily and watched her.

"Don't say that when Pamela's around." She put oil and vinegar in a screw-top jar, seasoned it and gave it to Harry to shake. "No, actually I was busy for most of the day. I'm afraid Colin called in."

"So?" Harry looked up, his blue eyes sharp and bright. "He's not bothering you, is he?"

"He is really." Kendall took the dressing back and poured it over the mixed salad bowl. "I don't know why he ever had to fall in love with me."

"He'd be crazy if he didn't!" Harry returned like a proud father.

"He's always been so quiet and gentle!" she exclaimed, "now he can't even speak calmly."

"The young idiot!" Harry selected a dressing-coated radish and ate it. "I'll have a word with him."

"If you ask me," Kendall couldn't stop herself saying it, "his mother's opposition is egging him on. She desperately wants him to fall in love with Sue Lockhart."

"I never!" Harry gave a rumbling laugh full of irony. "Since when do we fall in love to order?"

"You can say that again!"

"That sounded pretty wretched?" Harry looked up quickly into her troubled face.

"Did it?" She wasn't ready to take up the challenge.

"You don't love anybody yourself, do you?" Harry asked shrewdly. "Someone called Nick."

"Wouldn't *that* be a disaster!" she shrugged.

"I'm not so certain about that." Harry sat for a moment quietly, just watching his daughter's face. "Nick is a fine man. The best."

"You can't be serious, Harry!" She tried remarkably hard to smile. "Nick is a sophisticated man of the world, I'm eighteen years old."

"You'll be nineteen in August, you know."

"That's still too young for Nick. I couldn't match him in any way."

"I wouldn't worry about it if I were you," Harry said.

"Why not?" She moved to the cupboard and set out the plates.

"He's not marrying anyone else—that's the important thing. It seems to me, Nick's always been pretty fond of you. Many's the time he's chatted your own father up."

"He's got a great sense of responsibility," Kendall

pointed out. "You have to remember we were pretty green when we came up here."

"Still are." Harry laughed. "Farming is a full-time profession and any attempt of mine has only ended in shambles."

"All right. One glass of white wine," Kendall said, and handed the bottle to Harry to open.

"Are you going to join me?" Harry stood up, contemplating the bottle with a mournful expression.

"Why not?" she said lightly. "A glass each."

They sat down to their meal, ate the fresh salad, drank the cool wine. "Of course you've been in love with Nick since you've been fourteen years old," Harry said without looking up.

"Harry, you're crazy!" She said it almost hysterically.

"Strangely enough I've never been jealous." Harry ignored her frenzied protest. "I've always known the time would come to surrender up my little daughter, and all things considered we're not going to do any better than Nick."

"Oh, Harry!" Kendall suddenly bent her head, her forehead nearly touching the table. Her delicate shoulders were shaking, slightly at first, then heaving.

"Darling, you're not crying?" Harry jumped up in alarm.

She shook him off.

"Why you little wretch, you're laughing!" Harry said.

"Of course I'm laughing!" She looked up quickly, but her eyes were brilliantly close to tears. She looked enchantingly young and vulnerable, refusing to admit to her closest held secret. So secret, in fact, Harry had discovered it before she had. "You're priceless!"

"I'm right, though, aren't I?" Harry sat down again, as solid and reassuring as the Rock of Gibraltar.

"In a way." She tried a light smile, but it had a new

knowledge of pain in it. "Everyone has to have a first crush to remember."

"Poor child!" Harry sighed in deep understanding. "Some people leave a mark on our lives we can never erase. You see, darling, they belong!"

HOURS later, a minute before midnight precisely, Kendall stood restlessly at her window contemplating the night sky. What her father had said to her stuck in her mind. Pamela, for all she was part of their life, had never belonged. And the sad part was, she had always known it. At least, now, she had a consuming interest, but could it ever make up for the fact that she wasn't truly loved?

It would matter terribly to me, Kendall thought. To love and be loved was the most important thing in the world. It gave significance to everything. She returned in her memory to the sweet, vivid days when her mother had been alive—such a rush of memories, the tears gathered in her eyes. Life had been so meaningful then for Harry. Jokingly he had always called her mother a tyrant, then when she protested, hurt, he had always gathered her into his arms and called it "the sweetest tyranny of all." Kendall remembered the love between them, the laughter and the sharing. Even their arguments had so much love in them they produced the opposite effect, returning in memory as something to laugh about. Harry with his bear-hugs, her exquisite little mother with her head resting back on his chest and her slender pale arms resting touchingly over his strong, twined arms. *They* had belonged.

The knowledge brought with it a sudden wave of sadness such as she had not experienced since her mother died. Death was unalterable, final. But the love was undying. Harry had never found the same strength and happiness again. He had tried a new start with Pamela, but Pamela wasn't the kind of woman to enrich his life.

She loved him; there were all degrees of loving, but it wasn't the deep, unselfish love he had known.

Poor Harry! Much as she was determined to comfort him and offer him the greatest possible stability, he was really lost in a dream of the past. The moonlight touched her face and it looked strained and full of doubt. The truth was, Harry didn't really care that he was ruining his once splendid constitution. Didn't he often say he was "ready to give the game away"? Nick called it the other side of the coin, Harry's manic-depressive moods. It would be dreadful to be married to someone who meant the world to one and then lose them, damaged for ever. Maybe she had better accept it and stop telling herself and Harry he only had to work at it to make a success of his marriage. She had to accept what Nick had said to her; some loves were indestructible, unique. Deeply in love herself and grasping its torment, she suddenly understood Harry's restlessness, his loneliness, the hidden, festering wound. He was never without his small ghost, just waiting for her to put her arms around him just like the old days.

Kendall threw herself on the bed and wept bitterly— for Harry, for her mother, and for a third person who had penetrated to her very heart.

Nick.

PAMELA returned at the weekend, in high spirits and more glamorous than ever. Normally a very indolent person, she seemed full of energy and refused to stay in. She and Harry would go out to dinner.

"I don't think I want to," Harry said a little plaintively. "Can't we just have dinner at home?"

"No, we can't!" Pamela said firmly. "The trouble with you, Harry, is you've settled into a terrible rut."

"I've been working all day."

"If you mean painting," Pamela laughed gaily, "I don't call *that* work."

"Well, I can tell you it *is*." A muscle beside Harry's mouth was jerking.

"Please come, darling," Pamela tried to adjust to his mood. "It's important now for me to be seen."

"Ah, yes!" Harry remained in his chair and Kendall, who had overheard this exchange as she was dressing to go out herself, decided she had better intervene. It wasn't a good position to be in, but she was stuck with it unless she moved out. It was easy to understand Pamela's desire to go out and have a good time; on the other hand, Harry had been working steadily all day on his painting of Domino and he looked tired.

"Ah, there you are!" Harry said as though her intervention was going to let him off the hook. "You look lovely."

"That you do!" Pamela agreed unexpectedly. She seldom passed a comment about Kendall's appearance unless it was to blast some outfit or other.

"What are you two going to do?" Kendall turned right around to show Harry how her skirt floated.

"Nothing, I hope," Harry groaned. "What do you call that?" He looked at her chiffon dress with its gold leaf embroidery.

"China red." Pamela answered for Kendall, a little sharply. "It suits you beautifully with your black hair and gold skin. I've brought back some gorgeous Oriental gear. The Eastern look is pretty big down south. It would have been an idea, Kendall, to dress your hair more appropriately."

"I like it down," said Harry. "All swinging around her face. Most men would."

"You're so primitive, Harry," Pamela sighed. "The hair-do is very important to the line. I have a wonderful outfit I intend to wear tonight and I'm warning you now, my hair-style will be fairly exotic."

As though that settled the matter, she swept away, not giving Harry the opportunity to protest again.

"Never mind, darling," Kendall patted his shoulder consolingly. "Life is full of sacrifices."

"Blast!" Harry stood up. "Blast it!"

"You need some relaxation." Kendall looked up at him quickly. "You've really been *going* at that painting."

"And it's all but finished." Harry rubbed his eyes. "I don't think I could have done much better."

"I don't think so either." She put her arms around him and hugged him. "In fact I take good care not to get too close to the canvas in case he kicks me."

"Nick should be pleased." Harry breathed a sigh of satisfaction. "I didn't really want *Stampede* to go to the States even if the Yanks are crazy about that kind of thing, but this painting of Domino makes up for it. I intend to make a present of it to Nick."

"It'll be difficult," said Kendall. "You know he'll want to pay you."

"I think he's done enough for us all." Harry's rugged face was suffused with a gentle appreciation. "Make no mistake about it, nothing could shake my friendship with Nick, and I believe he has a very special regard for us."

Kendall nodded, not knowing what else to do. She didn't want to talk about Nick tonight when she had to fill in an evening with Dave Masterson. Now just the mention of his name had filled her with pathetic longings. Damn Nick and his hold on her!

Dave arrived about fifteen minutes later and when he saw Kendall's slender figure walking towards him, he whistled appreciatively. "Say, you look gorgeous!"

"Ran it up myself!"

"Really?" Dave looked as if he was prepared to believe anything of her.

"Hey, that's a joke!" she smiled at him. "This is a Pamela Paige model."

"Don't shop anywhere else." Dave took her face

gently between his hands and kissed her on the tip of the nose. "I'll say goodnight to your folks, then we'd better go. I have the table booked for seven-thirty."

Pamela was too deeply engrossed in her preparations to reappear as a super geisha to be interrupted, so Harry saw them off.

"We'll probably have a beastly time," he muttered for Kendall alone. "I detect exaggeration and a lot of guck."

"Promise me you're going to relax." There was a sudden undertone of anxiety in Kendall's voice. "You know what the doctor said. You've got to learn how to relax. Meditate."

"In the middle of my soup?"

"Well, not then," Kendall didn't smile. "But now, before you go out. Pamela's in such high spirits, it would be a pity to let her down."

"All right, darling," Harry kissed her cheek. "I'll go inside and relax every muscle, one by one. It's all agreed. Goodnight, Dave," he lifted his hand in salute.

"Goodnight, sir." Dave, who had been standing by the car door, opened it for Kendall to slip in. He had been telling himself unsuccessfully for a few weeks now that he didn't want to become seriously involved with any girl yet he had a horrible feeling Kendall could be "the one." It was insane to settle down at his age, yet when she looked up at him with those brilliant green eyes he didn't give a hang.

All through the evening, though Dave didn't want to be anywhere else, he had the feeling Kendall was worried. There was a tension in her lovely face even when she was smiling and he couldn't quite account for it.

"What's wrong?" he asked gently as they waited for coffee.

"Why, nothing." She looked across at him with swift apology. "Aren't I being good company?"

"The best," Dave replied simply, "but I have a feeling you've got something on your mind."

"I suppose we all carry around our little burdens," she said quietly.

"At your age?" He was seized with the desire to protect her, she looked so small and slender.

"At any age," she smiled at him. "Haven't you got any problems?"

"No," said Dave. "Unless it's getting you to keep on going out with me."

"Then you're lucky," she answered seriously.

"All right," Dave said purposefully. "I've got to do something to cheer you up. What about if we dance?"

"Love to!" Kendall made a determined effort to snap out of it, throwing back her head and lifting her delicate, bare shoulders.

"Gosh, you're beautiful!" Dave sighed.

They were out on the dance floor when she saw Nick standing just inside the entrance, talking to the head waiter. Both men turned their heads abruptly in the direction of the dance floor, and something about Nick's sombre expression struck at her heart. He looked very serious, looking intently about the crowd.

When his eyes rested on her, they seemed to burn her like coals and she turned out of Dave's arms and muttered, "Dear God!" aloud.

"What *is* it?" Dave looked down at her in utter perplexity, but she didn't even hear him. She was moving swiftly away from him as though programmed and he just caught the incomprehensible agony on her face. It was frightening, and he followed her off, only in that moment catching sight of Nick. Dave didn't dare guess what he was here for, but from the expression on his face it had to be something serious.

"Nick?" Kendall put her hands out involuntarily and Nick caught them.

"You'll have to come with me." There was an eerie pallor under his darkly bronzed skin.

"Harry?" she asked, like a desperately frightened child.

"They've taken him to the hospital." Nick lifted his head and looked at Dave. "Fix up here, will you, Dave? I'm taking Kendall to her father."

"He's alive?" Dave croaked, feeling crushed by Kendall's grief.

Nick nodded gravely. "A heart attack. It took some time to find you."

"Oh, God!" Dave couldn't even bring himself to think how he would feel had it been his own father. "I'll get Kendall's purse and follow in my car." He didn't want to intrude, neither did he feel he should go away.

Nick simply lifted his hand in acknowledgment and drew Kendall away.

All the way to the hospital she kept her eyes closed and Nick never spoke. What was there to say anyway? She had to keep quiet to pray. Harry had had a heart attack at the Club and Pamela, distraught, had rung Nick almost immediately. It had been her great good fortune to find him at home, for it had been up to Nick to find Kendall. Preoccupied as she had been with her own preparations for going out, Pamela hadn't bothered to ask where Kendall and Dave were dining and Harry, unconscious, had been unable to tell her. Dave's parents were out when Nick rang, but finally he had reached them at the home of a mutual friend. Mrs. Masterson had been able to tell him the name of the restaurant she herself had recommended to her son for the night's outing. After that, it took Nick hardly half an hour to find her.

At the hospital they found Pamela close to collapse. She had been crying and her starkly white face was adorned with black streaks of mascara.

"Oh, God, Nick!" She jumped up and grasped his arms. "They won't let me see him!"

"Keep calm, Pamela," he held her firmly by the shoulders, "he's in good hands."

"Dear God, don't let him die!" Pamela abandoned herself to her despair.

"Please, Pamela, sit down," said Nick, and eased her back on to the padded bench. "Kendall?" he turned his dark head swiftly, watching her press her hand to her mouth and bite on her fingers so she wouldn't cry.

"I'm all right," she said in a desperately controlled voice. "Have you got a handkerchief, Nick?"

He passed her a beautifully laundered, mono-grammed navy one out of his pocket and she leaned forward and gently wiped the mascara from beneath Pamela's eyes. "He's going to be all right," she whispered, wiping tears and mascara away.

Pamela caught her wrist. "I'm so frightened. He wanted to stay home and I *made* him go out."

"It's not your fault," she said sadly. "Never your fault."

"Sit down, Kendall." Nick was looking at her intently, realising she was close to collapse herself.

She nodded and sat beside Pamela, taking her hand. "Go and see if you can find out anything," she begged him. "They'll talk to you."

"They'll tell us when they're ready," Nick said. "I would only be in the way."

The minutes went past and still no one came near them. "You're taking this a damned sight better than I am!" Pamela accused Kendall almost hysterically.

Kendall was sitting infinitely still, tearless.

"I'm praying." She looked up and searched Pamela's eyes.

"Then stop!" Pamela flashed. "He's going to die."

"Enough!" Nick stood up abruptly, towering over

Pamela. "I'll get the nurse to give you something, Pamela. You're deeply shocked."

"I am." She jumped up as well, wringing her hands. "I didn't mean to shout at you, Kendall."

"I know."

"Come with me, Pamela." Nick put his arm around her shoulder. "I think you should lie down."

They disappeared up the corridor and a moment later Kendall saw Pamela being led away by a nurse.

She didn't want a sedative herself. She wanted to be fully alert to speak to her father. Nothing could take Harry from her and if someone didn't speak to her soon she would run up the corridor screaming.

A few seconds later Nick came back. He sat down beside her and gathered her into his arms.

"They've just told me."

He sounded, for the first time in all the years she had known him, unspeakably tired.

CHAPTER NINE

THREE dreadful months went by before Pamela announced that she had decided to move out of the farmhouse.

"I can't stand it any more," she told Kendall baldly. "I have to pick up my life. I have the business to consider. To be exact, it's been my salvation."

"Where will you go?" Kendall looked up at Pamela's tall, elegant body. She had grown very thin and indeed she was working incredibly hard.

"I thought I'd get myself a town house. Somewhere close to the shop."

"I'll help you in any way I can," Kendall told her, and looked out over the Lockharts' blossoming tea plantation.

"You already have." In an uncharacteristic display of affection Pamela laid her long-fingered hand on the side of Kendall's head. "I don't think I could have got through these last few months without you. You're a good girl, Kendall—strong."

"Not me!" Kendall shook her head without emotion. There was no emotion left in her.

"Perhaps, one day, you'll be a great lady," Pamela continued amazingly. "I'm different. I know I'll go quite mad if I stay here any longer, and I know you don't need *me* in any way."

"That's not true!" Kendall sought to reassure her.

"Oh, yes, it is." Pamela smiled a little bitterly. "You're the one who has been fussing over me all these weeks and making me eat. I've had no comfort to offer you because basically, I suppose, I'm rather a shallow person."

"*Please*, Pamela!" Kendall held up her hand, distressed. "If you don't want to stay here, I'd better sell the farm."

"Sell it if you want to." Pamela, too, looked out at the healing view. "I don't think you can continue to live here by yourself, but I certainly won't take anything from you. Your father left you all he had. I have the business. It's fair. One of these days I'll end up a rich woman and I'll have you to thank for coming up with the whole idea. I'd ask you to come and live with me, only I know we both want to be on our own."

It was undeniable. Their relationship had never gone very deep and without Harry they had very little in common.

"Have you already started looking?" Kendall asked.

"As a matter of fact I have." Pamela picked up her Italian leather bag. "If you stop by the shop about one o'clock I'd like to show you. You've no idea how much I miss you there," she added as she walked to the door. "Young Joanne hasn't got a fraction of your intelligence. I think I'll have to sack her."

"I wouldn't," Kendall called. "She brings all her friends in, remember? I suggest you hire another woman, an older, stylish lady. How about Sally Jamieson? I know she doesn't need the money, but I think she'd enjoy a few hours every day."

"Of course!" Pamela turned around and looked at Kendall as though she had dropped a brainwave. "Sally would be perfect, and she looks simply delightful."

"Then ask her."

After Pamela had gone, Kendall got up and began to clear away the breakfast dishes. She never felt hungry now, but if she couldn't manage to eat anything herself she would never have been able to persuade Pamela to keep her strength up. In her agitated state, Pamela had taken to chain-smoking and Kendall had devoted herself to helping her stepmother through a very bad period. Now, it seemed, it was over, and Pamela was ready to stand on her own.

Shortly before midday she dressed and drove into town and afterwards she and Pamela went to look over the townhouse in Park Street that overlooked the river. It really was very nice and Kendall was touched at how much Pamela wanted her to like it.

"We'll always be good friends, won't we, Kendall?" Pamela asked, sounding for the moment so sad, Kendall's insides were wrenched.

"Of course," Kendall smiled. "You're really lucky to find a place like this."

"*I* think so," Pamela agreed, starting to look brighter, "and it's so close to the shop." She directed her hand towards a new, modern apartment block further off to the right. "If you sold the farm you could buy one of those units. Perhaps not on the top, but a very good one. They all have a view."

"I'll think about it," Kendall said with no intention of doing any such thing.

She didn't linger in town but drove straight back to the farm, and as she swung in the front gate she saw Nick's car.

She thought she was past every sensation but grief, yet immediately her nerves began to jangle. In those early terrible days she and Pamela had been so shocked and bereft, they had had to rely heavily on Nick's active help and support, but for weeks now Kendall had retreated from Nick and everything he had once meant to her. From now on, she would keep carefully clear of loving. It only brought pain.

She parked her car underneath the house, but Nick didn't seem to be anywhere around. Unless he was in the house. He knew as well as she did where the door key was kept, on the beam to the left of the garage door.

The key was there, and as she got it down she saw Nick walking around the side of the house. Probably he had been looking around, about to tell her he was sending some men over to clear up the garden before it invaded the house.

"Hello, little one," he said gently, took her by the shoulders and kissed her cheek.

"Hello, Nick." She avoided his eyes like the plague. They demanded too much of her.

"Where have you been?"

"Oh, in town," she said evasively.

"Why?" he asked quietly. "Can't you tell me that?"

"I suppose you already know."

There was a dangerous fragility about her and it kept his voice quiet. "About Pamela?"

"She told you?" Somehow they were walking side by side into the enveloping quiet of the house.

"That she wanted to move out?" Nick moved away from her to look out over the magnificent view. "Yes, she did. I can't say I blame her. The house has some very unhappy memories."

"It doesn't bother me," Kendall returned brittlely. "Can I get you something, Nick?"

"I'll have a cup of coffee." He swung back to look at her and she noticed abstractedly how the stitching on his jacket matched his shirt.

"I'll get it." She put her bag down on the circular table and walked through to the kitchen, hoping Nick wouldn't follow her.

He did, his black eyes marking the deep melancholy of her expression and the way she was shivering slightly despite the sparkling sunshine. "You know you'll have to sell the farm," he pointed out seriously. "Jim Lockhart could add it to his property."

"You've got it all figured out, have you?" She put the lid on the percolator and set it on the stove.

"Don't you think you've been punishing me long enough?" he asked gravely.

"I don't know what you mean."

"Then *look* at me," he said quietly. "You never look at me any more."

"What's so terrible about that?" she asked raggedly. "The trouble with you, Nick, is you don't know when to leave well enough alone."

"I'm not leaving you alone," he said tersely. "And I'm especially not going to leave you alone in this lonely, ramshackle house."

"I like it," she said tautly. "If it bothers you just stay away."

"That's the difficulty—I can't." His beautiful mouth twisted. "I care about you, Kendall, you know that."

"Then there's precious little to care about!" She set the cups and saucers down jarringly. "When Harry went he took everything with him."

"You'll get over it, little one. You still have your wonderful memories."

"I'll never get over it!" she screamed at him. "Never. Never. *Never!*"

The unnatural calm that had protected her for so long shattered into fragments. She threw down a tea towel and raced from the kitchen, in her frenzy knocking over a favourite blue pottery vase that stood too near the edge of the dresser. She reached her room, slammed the door and flung herself on the bed. She was shaking violently and she hated Nick for bringing her to cruel life.

"Kendall!"

He followed her. She knew it. Nick, with his hard, unyielding core.

"Go *away!*" she muttered, and her voice broke.

"You must know by now I'm not going to do that." He said it very calmly, nothing emotional about it. "You need me, Kendall, only you won't admit it."

She didn't answer and he put his arm under her and turned her. "Would you marry me?"

"Why, Nick?" She stared at the ceiling.

"So I can look after you."

"I'd only make you miserable."

"I'm not laughing much now."

"Okay," she said, sounding dreadfully remote. "I'll marry you, but I won't love you."

"I'll remind you of that," Nick said abruptly, and didn't wait for her response.

THEY were married a month later. Not the big social event everyone had wanted and expected when Nick Langford married, but a very quiet private ceremony with only Pamela and Nick's closest family and friends.

Kendall hadn't really expected welcoming from Nick's family, but she found that she had it. Whatever anyone had hoped or longed for, if indeed they ever had, was now forgotten. The important thing was for Nick to be happy, and none of them questioned what went on behind Kendall's lovely, curiously still face. It was accepted beyond doubt that she was deeply in love with her husband and her gravity of manner was only natural in the light of her recent bereavement. Their marriage was commonly held to be a love match and everyone respected Nick's wish to have the girl he loved very safely in his care.

Only Kendall knew differently. The days of her honeymoon slipped by and though Nick was extremely attentive in public, his behaviour in private could scarcely be said to be love-like. It was back to Big Brother, with Nick jollying her through the hectically filled hours. Of necessity their time away from Flamingo Park had to be brief, so they spent little over a week jetting around three States, the days filled with sightseeing for Kendall, museums, art galleries, antique shops, and at night, the ballet, theatre and concerts.

He never gave her a minute to be alone with her thoughts.

In a way, it was a relief to be home. *Home*. Flamingo Park.

"Change anything you like," Nick told her.

What could she change? She was surrounded by perfection on all sides. Nick's mother, who had been so kind to her in the few days leading up to the wedding, was a woman of rare intelligence and taste. It didn't seem at all sensible to scrap any of her ideas. The only place Kendall could really turn to was the garden. There was so much of it surely no one would object if she took over a small area down by the fan palms, terrace it perhaps because it was on hillside and make it bloom with hundreds of little flowers, gazanias, zinnias, daisies, the ranunculus she loved. Hadn't Harry always admired her green fingers? She would create a garden for him.

They didn't share a bedroom, nor had they shared one in all the hotels they had stayed on their honeymoon. It came in handy, she thought coldly, to have a great deal of money. On the other hand she couldn't honestly say Nick had given the faintest indication that he wanted to share anything. He seemed perfectly content with the present arrangement. She had the most beautiful bedroom in the house—a woman's room warmed by gilded paneling, silk brocade and the finest French furnishings, while Nick occupied the rather overpoweringly resplendent suite that had been specially furnished for his grandfather.

Miraculously it worked. For some weeks Nick made no demands on her whatever—her time, or her attention. She came and went as she pleased, up very early to ride in the cool dawn, then supervising the two boys who were digging the terraces for her garden. Nick rarely came in for lunch and in the afternoon she swam or went riding again until it was cool enough to tend her garden again. It wasn't heaven, but she was surviving.

It surprised her then one night to have Nick come to

her bedroom. Once she had retired, he left her strictly alone.

"What is it?" she asked him, and her green eyes showed her sudden rush of fear.

"Just a little chat," he said dryly, and shut the door. "Are you happy here?"

"When I get used to such sumptuous surroundings." She turned away and reached for her peignoir.

"You manage all right!" His black eyes moved slowly over the picture she presented, mockery and a little violence in his gaze. No longer was she the little gypsy he once had known but a beautiful, exclusive-looking young woman. With her innate fairness she had done everything in her power to make herself look like Mrs. Nick Langford as long as he didn't lay a finger on her.

"I've heard from Liz," he told her in a spiked tone. "She wants to pay us a visit."

"Really?" Kendall turned her head and the light probed her fragile garments, revealing the curve of her shoulder, her tilting breasts, the narrow waist and the flow of her thighs into her beautiful slender legs.

"I knew you'd be pleased." Nick moved back and slumped into an armchair, looking extremely vivid and masculine against the delicate silk brocade. He was still in the same clothes he had worn at dinner and she didn't want to be forced to appreciate his striking good looks. Indeed she didn't want to look at him at all, yet he remained.

"Of course I'm pleased!" she said politely, shocked at the thought of coping with so many added complications. "Your mother was kind to me, very charming. This is her home."

"No, it's your home," he pointed out quietly, "even though you're just living here at the moment."

Something about his tone hurt her and she was taking such care to seal off her emotions. "I'm doing my best," she said poignantly.

"You'll have to do better," he said, gripping the sides of the armchair. "Liz would find it a little unusual to see us newlyweds so far apart. As a general rule, happily married couples share the same room. Forget the bed."

Agitation broke up her enforced composure. "Then it remains for you to think something up!"

"I already have!" His eyes narrowed over her. "There are countless rooms in this house. Your first job in the morning is to pick out a suitable bedroom for us both. We'll only stay there while Liz is here, of course. On my honour."

"I *won't*!" She stared at him, hating the brilliant mockery in his eyes.

"You made a bargain with me, remember?" His tone was light, yet it flicked her like a whip. "I've been handling you like a rare piece of porcelain and I'll continue to do so as long as you don't attempt to make a fool of me. My mother thinks we're deeply in love. I'm sure even you can appreciate what this means. We sleep together."

"You'll never get me to do that!" She had to rest back against the carved and gilded little writing table for support.

"Go on, it would be easy!"

"Considering your size and mine, you mean?"

His smile hardened. "I'm hoping it won't come to that."

"*Please*, Nick!" Her suddenly impassioned voice shocked even her. "Don't ask this of me."

"Why are you so afraid? God, *why*?" He almost sprang from the chair, gripping her shoulders. "You're creating some terrible problems for both of us. I've tried to be patient—God knows how I've tried."

"Stop, you're hurting me!" She made a pathetic attempt to pull free.

"At least you can feel *that*!"

She was trembling so violently his anger seemed to collapse and he drew her gently into his arms, running his hands up and down over her back as if she was a baby.

"Are you frightened I'll make love to you?"

"Yes." She couldn't stay where she was, crushed up against his heart.

"And you couldn't bear it?"

"You don't understand, Nick." She closed her eyes. "I want to be alone. All alone."

"Where no one can wound you?"

"Yes." She risked looking at him. "I'm sorry. You should never have married me."

A flash of anger crossed his dark face, but his voice remained cool. "Every man has a weakness," he said musingly. "You've been mine since you were fourteen years old. I've waited a damn long time, so even another year won't be anything special."

"I don't believe you!" Stunned, Kendall scanned the arrogant face above her, seeking the truth of his bold assertion. His expression was sardonic, with a dangerous winged slant to his brows.

"But then you're not very bright!" he said brutally, and put her away from him with cold detachment. "I'm sorry if it's going to turn you into a nerve case, but it happens to be true."

In the morning he was waiting for her and when she saw him, her stomach lurched. The thought of Nick touching her, any part of her, really sent panic fanning through her body. It was crazy. *She* was crazy. He couldn't want her as he said. It was just something he had made up, a fairy story for an impressionable child. A manoeuvre to get her to do what he wanted.

"You're going out?" she asked him, too shaken to challenge him in any way.

"Over to Colby Downs. They have a few problems. I might be able to help out."

She was still hovering on the staircase, with one hand

on the banister, so he crossed the floor and moved up to her on the stairs. "I'm absolutely serious about what I told you. Pick out a room. There's stuff galore in the attics—furniture, objects, everything. You might like to rummage up there. If you can't find what you want, then we'll get it in."

"Yes, Nick." She was too weary to contradict him.

"Good." He glanced at her indifferently. "I'll tell Liz we'll expect her in a week."

On the fourth day, when the last workman had moved out and the beautiful furniture was all arranged, Kendall sat alone on the huge, luxuriously draped bed and contemplated her future. The unnatural equilibrium of the last months had been completely destroyed. Almost overnight the insulation of grief had been stripped away and she was human again. Hurting, Nick, too, was different. The benign, always cool approach had gone. Now she was conscious that his black eyes followed her every move, noted every nuance of her voice, her every reaction. He was succeeding in turning her into a quivering mess.

She slipped her high-heeled sandals off and lay back on the beautiful bedspread staring up at the drapery. Had she really expected not to pay the ultimate price for marrying Nick? He was a man of strong passions, she knew that, yet she was forcing him into a situation where he could turn to somebody else. Still, she was violently frightened and tears flooded her eyes. If she gave in to Nick, surrendered up her heart even more than her body, she would leave herself open to a consuming passion. Nick was that kind of man.

Exhausted with her efforts and her sleepless, troubled nights, she drifted into a half waking dream. Nick was there beside her and all her shrinking would be in vain.

"Come on, baby, snap out of it!"

He *was* there, sitting on the bed beside her, and the

little whimpering sound she heard was coming from her own throat.

"I must have fallen asleep." She drew a shaky breath and pushed her tumbled hair away from her face.

"Only to dream about me."

"Right," she said feelingly.

"You're not looking forward to sharing my bed?"

She was going backwards in time when he made her every pulse race. "Surely you've heard of frigid women?"

Nick smiled faintly. "Heard of them, but I've never actually met one."

"Don't close your case-book yet." She made to get up, but he pushed her back gently.

"It seems a pity to waste an opportunity."

"No," she said.

"I'd be careful about that, too," he said. "The way you're always saying no." His hands closed around her waist and he leant over her. "I'm only going to kiss you. Nothing terrible, just a kiss."

He looked so careless and mocking, her heart turned in her breast. She didn't even attempt to turn away but lay quietly, and Nick brought his head down and covered her mouth with his own.

Liquid fire shot through her, burning her. It was getting harder and harder to lie still.

"I want to make love to you," he said quietly. "Okay?"

If I can't hear you, see you, this isn't happening to me, she thought.

"You like to put me through hell, don't you, Kendall?"

His voice held a mixture of anger, self-contempt and he made no attempt to touch her again.

ELIZABETH McFarland duly arrived, laden down with presents and so wonderfully warm and friendly Kendall found herself relaxing like a child in a mother's care.

"Why, I do believe you've lost weight, Kendall?" Her dark eyes flashed over Kendall's slight figure as she came to the dinner table. "You look absolutely beautiful, but we can't have you getting too fragile."

"It's all that gardening, I suppose." Nick bent a falsely anxious look on his young wife. "You wouldn't believe what she's done. Turned a barren hillside into an enchanting tropical garden."

"I'm proud of it." Kendall gave her husband a melting smile. If he could act, so could she.

"You'll have to show me in the morning," Elizabeth said. "I've always loved my garden. When you come down to us, you'll see all my camellias. I love camellias, don't you, dear?"

It was all surprisingly easy. The conversation ranged over so many subjects it kept Kendall on her toes and she came to see that now she lived in Nick's world she would have to turn into a cultivated woman. A woman like Elizabeth. It wouldn't be easy, but she was intelligent and quick to learn.

A little fatigued after the long flight, Elizabeth retired fairly early, delighted to be back in her old room. Nick had mentioned a dinner party Saturday night in her honour and she seemed touchingly pleased. Though she had been born into a wealthy family and had married a still wealthier man she was very appreciative of anything that was done for her, and Kendall had seen to it that there were bowls of her favourite roses placed in her room. Strictly speaking that was all she had to worry about; the floral arrangements. Mrs. Mitchell still ran the house very efficiently, so unobtrusive Kendall actually had to go looking for her rather than have her underfoot, and she departed to her own bungalow in the garden as soon as the dinner dishes were put away.

When Nick came to their new room she was piling cushions on the floor.

"What the hell are you doing?" he asked roughly.

"I'm sure you can figure that out." Her eyes were so big they dominated her face.

"You really kid yourself, don't you, darling?" He laughed gently and pulled off his shirt. "I don't want a shrieking little virgin on my hands. Not tonight."

"Great! Then I can have the bed." She took a running jump at it and tripped over the floating skirt of her cream chiffon nightdress. "Damn, damn, a thousand miserable damns!"

"Tell me, did that hurt?" Nick picked her up and threw her on the bed.

"Of course it did!" She bent over, clutching her elbow. "I don't know where you're going, Nick, but it's not in here." She didn't want to look at him, his bare torso and his dark, polished skin.

"Ah well, perhaps not," he said dryly. "I find it slightly unpalatable to rape my own wife."

"And that's what it would be," she hissed at him with great conviction. "Where will you go?"

"You've noticed the sofa in the dressing room, haven't you, darling?" The look he gave her should have made her cringe.

"But it's too small!" She measured his height incredulously.

"Not for you." He lifted her in one lunge and carried her through to the dressing room. "I dislike having to do this to you, but it's fairly obvious I need my rest."

"You brute!" She collapsed angrily on to the plush, cushioned sofa.

"Gently, darling, gently," he drew his hands from under her. "We don't want Mother to hear."

"I could easily hate you," she whispered violently.

"Thank you and good night," Nick walked purposefully to the door. "You won't mind if I shut this, will you? One must take certain precautions."

"*Lock* it for all I care!" she called moodily, and when

it was obvious he had done so, she shocked herself bitterly by bursting into tears.

At dawn she was awakened briefly when Nick lifted her and put her back into the big bed, warm from his body. He was dressed to ride out with the men and he told her, by means of shaking her by the shoulder, that he wouldn't be back until lunchtime.

Kendall slept deeply after that and when she finally went downstairs, a little pale and apologetic, Elizabeth was finishing off her breakfast, speaking cheerfully to Mrs. Mitchell.

"Ah, there you are, dear!"

"I'm so sorry, I slept in." Kendall smiled at Nora Mitchell, who returned the smile a little archly, then she went towards her mother-in-law. Elizabeth was one of those people it was very natural to kiss, and as Kendall bent to kiss the older woman's cheek, Elizabeth patted her arm with spontaneous affection. She was a very demonstrative woman with the people she loved and Kendall had been fascinated with the way she had rained kisses on Nick when they had met her at the airport.

"Come and sit down beside me," she said warmly, "there's so much I want to talk to you about. Nick's *wife*!"

The blood rose to Kendall's face and a faint shame moved in her. She was Nick's wife, all right, but only in name. She took her seat beside Elizabeth and when she glanced up found her brilliant black eyes on her face. Nick's eyes, beautiful, long-lashed. They were also deeply perceptive eyes, and Kendall resisted an impulse to pick up the newspaper and hide behind it.

"I know you're going to make Nick very happy, Kendall, and he cares very deeply for you."

"You don't think there's a little pity in it?" Kendall felt driven into asking, and to her surprise Elizabeth burst out laughing.

"My dear child, if you believe that, you'll believe anything!"

"I don't know," Kendall said softly. "It's very difficult to believe a man like Nick could love me."

"Surely he's proved it?" Elizabeth looked at her daughter-in-law closely. "Every young bride feels a little insecure. Give yourself time. You have so much to offer."

"Can you tell me something, Elizabeth?" Kendall asked.

"Surely, dear. Anything I can."

Kendall picked up her orange juice and put it down again. "Did you ever think Nick and Thalia would make a match of it?"

"Hardly." Elizabeth's shapely brows drew into a frown. "God knows we were all aware that Thalia hero-worshipped her cousin, but it never amounted to a problem. Why do you ask?"

"Thalia and her mother are back from their trip overseas. I imagine you'll want to see them on Saturday night?"

"Well, I don't think we can avoid asking them," Elizabeth pointed out. "I mean, they missed the wedding, and I'm very fond of Noel."

Kendall fell silent and Elizabeth looked at her with dark, understanding eyes. "Surely you're not worried about Thalia?"

"Not worried exactly," Kendall said evenly, though she felt her cheeks flush. "She dislikes me intensely."

"Maybe," Elizabeth said significantly, "but she won't be fool enough to show it. You're Nick's wife, and I think it's fairly obvious he's extremely protective of you. No one would dare to upset you while he's around."

"And I guess I can handle it when he's not."

"Of course you can!" Elizabeth patted her hand. "Remember, dear, I've known Thalia a lot longer than you have and it's not altogether her fault. Her mother spoilt her dreadfully—even Noel will admit that. She wanted Nick and she's been encouraged all her life to think she can have anything she likes. But believe me, dear, I know my own son. He's had scores of girls after him since he was sixteen years old, but he's only married you. Don't see a threat where there isn't one.''

THE smallish dinner party they meant to plan turned into a fairly large party. There were so many people, relatives and friends, Elizabeth said worriedly, one simply couldn't ignore. The word would go out and there would be the inevitable hurt. Why wasn't *I* invited? So between them, Elizabeth and Kendall, they made all the arrangements. Kendall need not have worried about being with her mother-in-law at all because Elizabeth was her kind of person and communication was effortless.

Nick noted it all but said nothing. As far as he was concerned his mother was magnificent, and such was her effect on Kendall that his forlorn little bride was beginning to look and act like her own self, her lovely clear laugh mingling with his mother's rich chuckle.

"Go away, Nick!" Liz often said to him. "We have to talk." He usually grinned mockingly and did just that. Elizabeth felt deeply about people and it was obvious she was encouraging Kendall to talk to her, as apparently Kendall was.

The arrangement in the bedroom still went on, but mercifully Elizabeth didn't know about that. Dressing for the party that evening Kendall had relaxed to the extent she didn't mind Nick wandering in and out at all. She was even a little excited, though she was constantly trying to calm herself down.

"You look very beautiful," said Nick, and before she could stop him, bent his head and kissed her bare shoulder.

She shivered a little and put her hand to her throat. "Thank you, Nick."

"Obviously sleeping on the sofa doesn't bother you." He lifted an eyebrow with dark mockery.

"Actually it's quite comfortable." She gave him a jewelled sidelong glance.

"I bet you don't know I kiss you before I pick you up and put you in my bed," he jeered lightly. "It's easy to cherish you when you look like a flower."

As she looked up at him, her own expression changed elusively. Just the look of him, all that splendid dark arrogance, was too much for her. She swayed slightly towards him and instantly he drew her hard up against him so she was conscious of the mounting tension within him.

"How long are you going to fight me?" he asked tautly. "I suppose you know we can't go on like this. You *must* know."

She sighed and rested against him, remembering when she had loved him with all her heart. "Please don't be angry with me, Nick."

"Angry—oh, boy!" He shrugged and laughed and lifted her chin with his fingertips. "Whatever you do, just remember, I do not intend to let you go."

All their guests seemed to arrive together and not a one of them wasn't fascinated by the emeralds Kendall wore around her throat and in her ears. If the truth were known, she was still dazed herself, for Nick had only given them to her tonight, his hands gentle as he touched her nape, and not so gentle as they swept over her breasts to her tiny waist.

The emeralds glittered with green fire, no greener than her eyes, a wonderful complement to her golden skin and the virginal white of her long dress with its tightly fitted strapless bodice. She looked rich and beautiful and Nick's word, cherished, but inside she was trembling and on the run from Nick's magnetic sensuality.

Thalia didn't arrive with her parents but to everyone's surprise made her appearance with Dean Hallitt, who had definitely not been invited.

"Kendall dear, you look stunning!" she cried, and from the hectic glitter in her eyes it was clear she had resorted to a few drinks for Dutch courage.

"Mrs. Langford!" Dean drawled, and kissed her hand. "Do forgive me for gatecrashing, but Thalia assured me you wouldn't mind."

Thalia was looking feverishly around the room for Nick, and Kendall, even with her back turned, knew the instant she spotted him, by the terrible flash of pain in her eyes. The pain of rejection and bitter jealousy. Kendall had the strong feeling that if Thalia could do her an injury, she would.

Elizabeth, catching sight of their strangely frozen tableau, seized the opportunity to rescue Kendall. She sailed up regally, apparently delighted to see her niece by marriage though she had never liked the girl no matter how she tried. She knew exactly how she felt about Dean Hallitt, but Thalia had outwitted them by bringing him along. After all, they could scarcely throw him out, and he was the only black sheep in his whole family.

The party went on for several hours and there seemed no way to relieve Thalia's pain. Because of her compassionate nature, Kendall felt sorry for her, even though other people, including her parents, were regarding her with mingled worry and dismay. Even Dean had told her to take it easy, but she gave him a brittle smile and emptied another glass. Finally, dutifully, her mother spoke to her and got nothing whatever for her trouble. Thalia saw no reason whatever to hide her feelings. She had loved Nick all her life, now some little farm girl had stolen him away.

Kendall, who had been trapped into dancing with Dean Hallitt, looked him full in the eyes. "I really think it would be best if you took Thalia home."

"Let her go," he drawled insolently. "She's rather amusing."

"Don't you care for her at all?" She gave him a stern look.

"Not right now!" He caught her even closer. "No man in his right mind would prefer Thalia to you."

"You're staring," she told him sharply.

"So? Everyone is tonight. Nick's little oddity has turned into a swan."

"I've never thought of myself as an oddity," Kendall said, "on the other hand, I think you're positively weird!"

"I'm used to it, darling," Dean shrugged. "My own parents don't talk to me."

"If you don't mind, I'm tired of dancing," Kendall said coldly. She wasn't choosing her words carefully as she might have been considering he was the type of man who thrived on unpleasant games.

"Frightened we'll make Nick jealous?" He wouldn't let her go. "Why did you have to go and marry him? You could have married me."

She wasn't sure how to proceed. Words would only inflame him, then she saw his eyes focus over her shoulder and his grip on her lightened and finally fell away.

"All right, Nick, I know," he said, flamboyantly throwing up his hands. "I mustn't monopolise your wife."

"There's something else you can do," Nick returned curtly. "You can take Thalia home."

"But this is the best night of her life!" Dean smiled unpleasantly. "The night she has to accept that you don't want her and never did."

Nick put his hand on the other man's shoulder and he kept his sickly smile, though the pain was excruciating. "I'd take it as an extreme favour if you'd leave. It would be easier all around."

"Well now, I suppose I'd better." Dean wasn't too

far gone that he didn't recognise his host's mood. Humiliation was at hand. "Don't expect me to take Thalia off your hands. I didn't want to come in the first place, but she made it worth my while."

"Get out," Nick said very quietly, but Dean knew exactly where he stood.

"Good evening, Mrs. Langford." He lifted his hand to Kendall in mock salute. 'Lovely party!"

She hardly heard him, Nick looked so dark and intimidating. "There are very many people here to be nice to," he said shortly. "I don't know how you can bear Hallitt."

"I detest him!" she gasped.

"Really?" He looked at her and there were strange, leaping lights in his eyes. "You've got some way of showing you detest a man."

"He wouldn't let me go." She looked up into his black eyes, almost pleadingly.

"Never mind—" He dismissed the whole thing abruptly. "I'll have to get Thalia home, before she makes a holy show of us all."

"Surely she's got a father?" Kendall was shocked at her sudden rush of jealousy.

"Who can't handle her any more than her mother can. I won't be long."

Through a haze Kendall saw him move away to where Thalia was standing just outside one of the open French doors. She saw Thalia lift her head to him with a brilliant, agonised smile, then he had his hand on her arm and they were moving back along the terrace to the drawing room.

By the time Kendall felt able to move inside, they were gone.

THE party went on until well after midnight; a good party marred by Thalia's pathetic behaviour. Everyone had felt the embarrassment, none more than her parents, who left a short time after Nick. Nevertheless he hadn't returned for an hour.

"Drat the girl!" complained Elizabeth, with an uncharacteristic lack of sympathy. "A perfectly good party ruined!"

"I'm sorry," Kendall murmured.

"But my dear, I'm mad on your account!" Elizabeth told her. "How dare she come here in that state! And that dreadful Dean! Honestly, he's creepy. It just might be an idea if you avoid him like the plague. He seems to find you too attractive."

"More's the pity!" Kendall said bitterly. "I hardly feel flattered." Nick hadn't spoken to her directly for the rest of the night.

"Thank God Nick got rid of him," Elizabeth said, and stood up. "I wouldn't have him in the house again."

"I wanted everything to be just right for you," Kendall gave her mother-in-law a pained look.

"But, my dear, I'm very, very happy!" Elizabeth embraced her. "These little irritations are only trifles. I came to get to know my daughter-in-law, and it's been a great pleasure."

"For me, too," Kendall said smilingly, which earned her another kiss.

"Ah, here's Nick!" Elizabeth glanced a little guardedly at her son. "All locked up?"

"We can all go to bed," Nick said almost grimly. "God, what a night!"

"No matter!" Elizabeth said brightly. "A lot of it was delightful. Now, my children, I'm going to bed. You won't see me before ten at the earliest."

Kendall reached their bedroom before Nick and she hovered in the middle of the room uncertainly. The impulse to lock him out didn't even cross her mind. Nick in a certain mood was capable of anything and he seemed tense and disturbed. Probably Thalia had wound her strong arms around his neck and refused to let go. Probably she had landed kisses wherever she could, provoking an unwanted, twisted excitement. Nick surely wasn't getting any kisses at home. The thought of Nick with another woman in his arms was unbearable. Though there had been a whole lot of women. Even Elizabeth had said so, and Kendall distinctly recalled several herself.

A little frantically she hunted up her nightclothes and went through to the adjoining bathroom and put them on. She couldn't release the catch on the emerald necklace and it looked outlandishly erotic with her satin nightdress. She tilted her head forward and tried again, swearing mildly under her breath. She couldn't get the hang of it. Nick would have to do it for her or she would have to go to sleep standing up.

Agitated now, she walked back into the bedroom, only to find Nick prowling around the room like a panther.

"I didn't quite realise you'd be undressed so soon." He swung on her, his glittery gaze slanting in unholy satire over her face and her slender body. "Is there a race or something? Break a leg to get into the dressing room?"

"Could you please take my necklace off?" she asked quietly, though her heart seemed to be going into spasms.

"Leave it there," he said insolently. "It looks fabulous." Recklessness lay on him like a brilliant patina and Kendall thought frantically any moment he would reach for her.

"I can't sleep in it, Nick?" she managed, low-voiced.

"And where in sweet hell is that?" he asked maliciously. "The sofa?" He looked dangerous, relentless, and suddenly she wanted to hit him and hit him hard.

"Don't take it out on *me*, because your cousin caused a scene!"

"*She* did!" His eyes struck grimly on her face. "Lady, you'd better explain yourself."

"Me?" she echoed tragically. "I've done nothing. It just makes you feel better to attack me."

"And why not?" he asked broodingly. "After all, I can take so much."

Her heart beats were so stormy now she was frightened and she even curled a hand over her heart.

"My terrified little wife," he said bitterly, and his white teeth snapped together.

"Oh, please, Nick, don't let's fight." She could sense the devil in him and she walked towards him, submissively bending her head. "Would you please help me with my necklace? I can't manage the catch."

"Dear God!" He shook his head a little helplessly and as she turned round, very small and slender, he gathered her back against him. "You know damned well I'm going to take you tonight."

"Maybe I want you to." She gave a strange little laugh. She could see their reflections in the long mirror and it made her pulses pound. Like someone awakening from a deep sleep she saw her husband and the superb excitement that enveloped him. She hadn't realised he was so dark, or his skin so deeply tanned, until she saw herself, a pale golden figurine locked beneath the semi-circle of his arms.

He brought his head down until he was murmuring in her neck. "Don't torment me with things you don't mean."

She felt as though a great cloud of ecstasy had clasped her in its wings, so when his hands possessed her breasts, she curled back against him and lifted her face thirstily, like a flower towards rain.

Nick seemed to draw a breath in agony, then he swept her up into his arms, both of their bodies burning in a fever that took the night to spend.

CHAPTER TEN

WHEN she awoke in the morning, she was naked and alone. She let her hand slide across the pillow, even now the blood drumming in her veins. Why hadn't she kept her arms around him, trapping him? Every inch of her body felt the thrill of his hands.

She sighed deeply, the memory of passion so recent she was still over stimulated.

"You're so beautiful," he had whispered, caressing her so deeply she had become wildly excited.

Didn't he know, didn't he feel that she loved him, her body convulsing, irrevocably lost to him. But he hadn't hurried anything, but drawn her on until she shot into space endlessly, the inarticulate little cry she made smothered by his mouth.

Nick!

A mad happiness filled her and a deep thankfulness. If this was surrender it was what she wanted all her life. For a few moments more she lay there, her young breasts pressing against the sheet. She wanted Nick so badly. Where was he?

She slid her hand out of bed and sought for her nightgown. She had no clear recollection of anything except the passion that had swept over them. She blushed suddenly, thinking there was nothing Nick didn't know about her now.

Her nightgown was hanging up. So was her robe. She had a sensation of splintered memories when she recalled how Nick had stripped them from her. She felt almost the same panic now as then. But the waves of wild desire had come on her, from which there had been no retreat.

An intense longing for her husband assaulted her. Had she once told him she loved him? It had been difficult for her to speak in that spinning world without beginning and end. Had *he* said those fateful words? She was still trying to remember.

"I'll never let you go." Nick's voice was low, tyrannical with possession. He had told her many times that he wanted her, demanding her response, but her emotions had been so aflame she had never found her voice.

She would tell him now. Today. Not only that, she would show him.

When she went downstairs Mrs. Mitchell was answering the phone in Nick's study. She heard her voice clearly. She heard her say: "I'll tell her."

Kendall stood in the entrance hall waiting. Her heart had begun to beat violently, an unpleasant sensation associated with the phone. What made such small things so difficult to bear was the memory of her suffering. The way the phone had rung when Harry died. She hated the phone. It never brought good news.

Mrs. Mitchell's round pink face was quite pale. She came right up to Kendall and put her hand on her shoulder. "There's been an accident, dear. As I understand it, probably not serious."

Kendall didn't say anything. She just stood where she was with all the soft colour draining away from her skin.

"Please don't panic, dear," Mrs. Mitchell urged. "Though I can understand it. Mr. Langford will be all right."

Still Kendall didn't reply and Mrs. Mitchell could see quite clearly she was thoroughly shocked.

"He *will*. Of course he will. It was rather stupid of Frank to ring with so little information." She got her arm around the girl and drew her into the study, putting her down in one of the leather armchairs. Then she took a quick determined look around for the brandy. Considering what the young Mrs. Langford had been through it was cruel to subject her to another shock.

She found the brandy, poured a little into a crystal tumbler and came back to Kendall. "Steady now," she said soothingly, and held the glass up to Kendall's mouth.

Kendall shook her head.

"I think you need it, dear. You're shaking."

"Nick!" Kendall whispered, her teeth chattering.

"What's wrong? What's happened?" Elizabeth was there, her eyes fixed on Kendall in concern. "Kendall, for God's sake, what's wrong?" She moved quickly to the armchair and knelt down in front of the shaking girl.

"N...N...ick!"

"Go easy." Elizabeth looked up and raked Mrs. Mitchell with her eyes. "What's happening here?"

"There was a phone call," Mrs. Mitchell told her, taking short, gulping breaths. "From Frank. At least I think it was Frank. He was so rattled. There's been some kind of accident at the stables—one of the horses. Domino."

"And Nick?" Elizabeth looked agonised. "So *tell* me, for God's sake!"

"I don't know, ma'am." Nora Mitchell's eyes filled with tears. "All he said was there's been an accident and I was to tell Mrs. Langford."

"Damn it all, he probably meant *me!*" Elizabeth muttered distractedly. "He *couldn't* worry Kendall."

"Domino is dangerous," Kendall suddenly announced in a frightful little voice. "Nick always spoke of the risk."

"I'll have to go down." Elizabeth had aged ten years.

Immediately Kendall jumped up and looked around

the room with blind eyes. "God couldn't do this to me, could He?" she asked.

"Now, dear, *now*!" Elizabeth gathered her into her arms. "We really don't know what's happened at all."

"Then we must go." Kendall forced her head up, though she was shockingly white.

There was the sound of a vehicle being driven right up to the entrance, the slam of a door, then a man's footsteps racing up the marble stairs.

"I'm so *afraid*!" Kendall whispered, and her legs buckled under her.

If Elizabeth had not been strong Kendall would have fallen to the ground, then like a miracle, the most wonderful miracle of her life, Nick was there.

"Oh, God, darling, you're not hurt, are you?" Elizabeth demanded, her dark eyes dilating.

"No, no." He took his wife out of his mother's arms, lifted her off her feet and cradled her in his arms. "It was the most terrible mistake. Domino lashed out and savaged one of the stable boys. I've told them repeatedly to leave the handling of the stallion to Ray Huntley, but there's always one who won't listen."

"Is he all right?" Elizabeth slumped weakly into a chair and Mrs. Mitchell hurried off to make tea.

"I sure hope so." Nick too collapsed into an armchair, holding tightly on to Kendall, who was clinging to him feverishly. "You wouldn't believe the job I had getting Domino back into his box."

"I can just imagine," Elizabeth shuddered, acutely aware of how frighteningly dangerous stallions could be. "You'll have to geld him."

"No." Nick shook his head emphatically. "That would be a crime. Jimmy actually asked for trouble, the young fool. Domino isn't deadly, only dangerous when provoked. Maybe now the boy will take my orders seriously. Frank has taken him to the hospital for a

thorough check-up. He's bruised and he's bitten and he's certainly had his collarbone broken.''

"We thought it was *you*,'' Elizabeth said finally.

"So did Frank.'' Nick's hand was tangled in Kendall's hair and her face was buried against his chest. "It was the night watchman who made the call. Usually he's very sensible and reliable, but he didn't get a thing straight. Frank asked him to say there'd been an accident on the morning round of inspection so I wouldn't be back to the house, but apparently he thought I'd been injured and passed that on as well.''

"Well, I find that appalling,'' Elizabeth exclaimed. "He put us through hell!''

"Kendall?'' Nick got his hand under her chin and lifted her face to him. "My poor little girl!''

"Take her back to bed,'' said Elizabeth. "I think I'll lie down myself. I'm quite faint with relief.''

Up in their bedroom Nick lowered Kendall gently on to the bed and sat down beside her chaffing her wrist.

"If I could get hold of poor old Ted now, I'd choke him. As it was, he was deeply upset. I suppose rounding the corner and seeing me stooping over Jimmy he didn't know for sure who'd been injured.''

"Don't talk about it,'' Kendall pleaded, and shuddered in remembered horror. "I thought it might have been my punishment.''

"For what, darling?'' Nick lifted her hand and kissed the upturned palm.

"For not telling you I love you.''

"Didn't you tell me last night?'' His voice was very deep and beguiling.

"I couldn't be sure.'' She gripped his hands and pressed them to her face. "It was all so dazzling. When I woke up this morning, I longed to tell you how I felt, but you weren't there.''

"I'm sorry.'' He bent his head and gave her a kiss of

great tenderness and passion. "Did I tell you I loved you?"

"Never." Her eyes reflected her deep hunger.

"I should have told you a million times," he said quietly. "But love isn't always kind. With me, it's been a mad, consuming fire. I loved you when I first saw you and I love you now. I'll always love you. The infernal thing was, I didn't know exactly your feelings for me. Last night you let me love you in every way I wanted and it was magic but this morning when I looked at you curled up beside me, I began to feel remorse. You're so young. So desperately young sometimes, I thought I might have driven you into surrender. After all, I have to admit my desire for you is boundless. Last night swept us both away, but this morning I doubted myself."

"You did?" Swiftly she moved, linking her arms around the strong tanned column of his throat. "The great Nick Langford doubted himself?"

"Can't you see that I might?" His black eyes were blazing, brilliantly alert.

"But I love you dreadfully!" she said tragically, and leaned her head against his chest. "I love you so much, I'm half mad with it."

"Good." Nick laughed in his throat and tightened his hold on her. "It'll be delightful to have you as my little slave."

"I think it unlikely!"

She heard Nick's low laughter, then he turned her head up smoothly, and with natural mastery kissed her mouth.

Harlequin Romances

The books that let you escape
into the wonderful world of romance!
Trips to exotic places…interesting
plots…meeting memorable people…
the excitement of love….These are
integral parts of Harlequin Romances—
the heartwarming novels read by
women everywhere.

Many early issues are now available.
Choose from this great selection!

Choose from this list of Harlequin Romance editions.*

Some of these book were originally published under different titles.

Relive a great love story...
with Harlequin Romances
Complete and mail this coupon today!

Harlequin Reader Service

In U.S.A.
MPO Box 707
Niagara Falls, N.Y. 14302

In Canada
649 Ontario St.
Stratford, Ontario, N5A 6W2

Please send me the following Harlequin Romance novels. I am enclosing my check or money order for $1.25 for each novel ordered, plus 59¢ to cover postage and handling.

☐ 422	☐ 509	☐ 636	☐ 729	☐ 810	☐ 902
☐ 434	☐ 517	☐ 673	☐ 737	☐ 815	☐ 903
☐ 459	☐ 535	☐ 683	☐ 746	☐ 838	☐ 909
☐ 481	☐ 559	☐ 684	☐ 748	☐ 872	☐ 920
☐ 492	☐ 583	☐ 713	☐ 798	☐ 878	☐ 927
☐ 508	☐ 634	☐ 714	☐ 799	☐ 888	☐ 941

Number of novels checked @ $1.25 each = $ _____

N.Y. and Ariz. residents add appropriate sales tax. $ _____

Postage and handling $ _____ .59

TOTAL $ _____

I enclose _____
(Please send check or money order. We cannot be responsible for cash sent through the mail.)

Prices subject to change without notice.

NAME _____
(Please Print)

ADDRESS _____

CITY _____

STATE/PROV. _____

ZIP/POSTAL CODE _____

Offer expires September 30, 1981.   102563371